SKY TRAIN

SKY TRAIN

And Other Ward Stories from CBC's Fresh Air

WARD MCBURNEY

Oct. 24 2019 - aged 57

Foreword by Jeff Goodes

DUNDURN PRESS
TORONTO · OXFORD

Editor: Dennis Mills
Design: Bruna Brunelli
Printer: Transcontinental

Canadian Cataloguing in Publication Data

McBurney, Ward
  Sky train: stories from CBC's Fresh air

ISBN 1-55002-359-4

I. Title.

PS8575.B87A16 2001   791.44'72   C2001-902112-7   PR9199.3.M285A16 2001

1   2   3   4   5   05   04   03   02   01

Canada

THE CANADA COUNCIL | LE CONSEIL DES ARTS
FOR THE ARTS | DU CANADA
SINCE 1957 | DEPUIS 1957

ONTARIO ARTS COUNCIL
CONSEIL DES ARTS DE L'ONTARIO

We acknowledge the support of the **Canada Council for the Arts** and the **Ontario Arts Council** for our publishing program. We also acknowledge the financial support of the **Government of Canada** through the **Book Publishing Industry Development Program**, **The Association for the Export of Canadian Books**, and the **Government of Ontario** through the **Ontario Book Publishers Tax Credit** program.

Care has been taken to trace the ownership of copyright material used in this book. The author and the publisher welcome any information enabling them to rectify any references or credit in subsequent editions.

J. Kirk Howard, President

[Photo credits]
All images are from the author's collection, unless otherwise indicated:
Cover, pages 105 and 125: Jim Panou; page 17: City of Toronto Archives, RG 8, Series 6, Item 22.

Printed and bound in Canada.⊛
Printed on recycled paper.

www.dundurn.com

Dundurn Press
8 Market Street
Suite 200
Toronto, Ontario, Canada
M5E 1M6

Dundurn Press
73 Lime Walk
Headington, Oxford,
England
OX3 7AD

Dundurn Press
2250 Military Road
Tonawanda NY
U.S.A. 14150

In memory of
Helen Jean McBurney
1929–1997
Teacher, Mother, Beloved

"& the whole garden will bow"

— *e.e. cummings*

CONTENTS

ACKNOWLEDGEMENTS

It is impossible to thank all the people who contributed towards this book. This otherwise welcome task is made all the more difficult by the nature of my work: each story draws a circle of friends and colleagues around it, some emphatically acknowledged in its lines, most not.

My father, Ernest Reginald McBurney, is the best man I will ever know. My brother, Blair, is entirely responsible for my great fame at the Mississauga Central Library. Eva-Marie Stern saved the life that is the vehicle for these pages. Bruce Cane and Shelley Wall have been the stories' most constant and immediate readers — nothing gets out that does not go by their careful and loving eyes. Siobhan McMenemy has promoted the project of my textual life in more ways than I can name. Mychol Scully lifted me up to speak in Toronto when all I could do was mumble into my sleeve. Jim Panou's expertise, generosity, and vision informs the cover and all the images in this book. Jim Ormond is my literary father.

Particular and irreplaceable support (and the high-handedness of putting these superlative individuals — none of whom appear in the stories themselves — in a *list* is not lost on me) has been given by Susan Aihoshi, Rick Archbold, Richard Bachmann, Dana Bailey, Ronna Bloom, Elgin Cleckley, Jennifer Donnelly, John Flannery, Chris Garbutt, Bethany Gibson, Susan Goldberg, Kevin Hebib, Frank Herr, Beth Kaplan, Sandra Kleinfeld, Jennifer Levine, Allan Luffman, Andrea McIntyre, Amy Nelson-Hahn, James Michael Ramsay, Rosemary Shipton, Cathy Swire, Lora Tamburri, Germaine Warkentin, Juliet Warkentin, and Nancy Weiler.

How many writers are given the right venue, time after time, and are blessed with the best people there to work with? Jeff Goodes and Barb Dickie, host and producer of *Fresh Air*, respectively, are two of those, as are the big voice and heart of Adrian Schuman; behind them also stand Dwight Friesen, Chris Hope, Michelle Parise, Carol Warren, and of course Tom Allen, who began this series by inviting me to write in to the show, when he was host.

And how many writers find the right publisher at the right time, when their typescript is ripe in their hands? Kirk Howard and Beth Bruder of Dundurn Press both deserve my heartfelt thanks for taking a chance on me, as do Barry Jowett and Kerry Breeze for shepherding and promoting the book. Bruna Brunelli turned out the nicest pages I have seen since Gallimard's edition of *L'Étranger*.

Many friends gave their time and attention reading these stories as emails sent out before broadcasts and praised or propped up my fledgling work, my book *in statu nascendi*. Lastly, I would like to thank all those who tune in to *Fresh Air*, and who listen to my stories, in kitchens, automobiles, and (not infrequently) bed: without your attention, nothing that follows, follows.

FOREWORD

On a sunny Saturday morning, Ward and I were heading down the QEW enroute to the Niagara Bike Trail. Ward is an excellent travel partner. He's pretty much a walking, talking historical plaque — particularly in an area of the country rich with stories of the War of 1812.

On a generic stretch of the highway near Oakville, we drove by a big yard sale sign stuck on a chain-link fence. Behind the fence set back a good distance was a red brick farmhouse, out of place in this suburban landscape. It looked like they were doing a pretty good business, cars were crowding down the dirt lane in search of bargains.

"I can't believe it," Ward shook his head. "That's the last farmhouse on the QEW between Toronto and Hamilton. I bet they finally sold out. They'll probably build something like that." He pointed to a twelve-storey mirrored office building across the highway.

A moment of silence. Then a heavy sigh. "I have a real problem with progress."

I describe Ward's stories as coming from a place where the past and the present dance together.

Ward comes in Saturday mornings to read his stories on *Fresh Air*, CBC Radio One's weekend morning show here in Ontario. No matter the season, he gets up early and sets out on foot from his home at a co-op on Toronto's waterfront. He meanders through the deserted streets as the city stretches into morning. I say "meanders" because he is rarely early and sometimes late ... and because I imagine that the city Ward sees is very alive despite the early hour.

When he leaves his home and looks south to the lake's edge, there is William Ward, caked in ice, dragging survivors from a sinking ship to the shore.

He climbs the hill to the Bathurst Street Bridge aware that at some point in time, the entire iron structure was picked up and moved when the street changed direction. As he crosses its cobweb of girders, he catches a glimpse of a streamlined train, a powerful steam engine pulling a line of emerald passenger cars on the elevated track.

On Front Street, I'm sure he notices sepia shadows of drunken garrison soldiers, uniforms rumpled, staggering down to their barracks at Fort York, pausing to throw up on the steps of Planet Hollywood.

When he gets to the Broadcasting Centre, he sees it as just the latest layer of the City, built on top of railroad tracks, taverns, vegetable gardens, and campsites.

Don't get me wrong though. Ward isn't a soppy sentimentalist. His stories don't just deal with the past, but with possibility too. We are adding our own echoes to the dust heap of history. And soon it will all be left for someone else to sift through. Someone pondering the continuum of community.

Someone just like Ward.

Jeff Goodes
Host
Fresh Air
CBC Radio One

INTRODUCTION

A good friend took his life some time ago. When it happened, it was the fall, and I was in New York City, studying acting. I didn't hear about it, however, until I came home for Christmas.

"How's Mike?" I had asked, at the home of another friend, who lived in Kensington Market in downtown Toronto.

"You mean you don't know?" she replied.

I remember running out to catch the streetcar, arriving in the guardroom at Historic Fort York, where Mike (and I) had worked, and asking my assembled mates and co-workers "Is this true?" And so they all had to relive that loss, then and there, at the site where it had happened a month before.

When it came time to write a piece of that event for *Fresh Air*, I was more trepidatious than usual. I ran the story past Jeff Goodes, the host, as I always do. Aside from chopping off the first two paragraphs (they were in the way; Jeff has great narrative sense), he had no problems with it. I then ran it past Bruce Cane, who had been in the guardroom when I burst in, and who hovers over all these stories, as he did me on that heavy day. Lastly, I sent the piece to the curator of Fort York, Carl Benn. Carl likewise had no objections, but wondered, What would Mike's family think?

That gave me pause. I had never had any contact with his family. Nor, it turned out, had any of my old friends from the fort. There were a lot of people with Mike's last name in the phone book. I couldn't just call them up randomly asking if they'd lost a son. Besides, wasn't the story, as I told it, mine? Was it not a eulogy, long overdue — the one I never gave, vaulting skyscrapers in Manhattan? I performed the piece ("Mike's Drum") live, in the studio, as Jeff has taught me to do, just after the eight o'clock news on Saturday morning, 19 February 1999.

Six months later, I received the following email:

Dear Ward:

I am writing to you regarding a Fresh Air broadcast earlier this year.

On February 19 I woke up and just happened to turn on the radio. I was lying in bed half asleep listening to your story when about halfway through I realized you were talking about my brother Mike. It was such an incredible experience because when I initially woke up before turning on the radio, the first thing I thought was that it would have been Mike's 40th birthday that day (I don't know if you knew that or if that was a coincidence).

Then I heard your story. I was lying in bed staring at my radio, riveted. It was pure luck that I happened to hear the story, otherwise I would have never had any idea you wrote it or knew him. Or maybe it was fate that I heard it and was just meant to happen.

Thank you for what was a truly wonderful experience.

Sincerely,
Doug ———

It *was* a coincidence. And as Doug makes clear, the stories are not entirely mine, after all. They are given me to speak, they seem to find their own audiences (as Jeff often says, "You can never tell who's listening"), and they participate in something greater than my desire to splash down over the airwaves of Ontario. There have always been stories to the stories; the happenstance way they assemble and spur themselves has always been, for me, a narrative in itself, running alongside the emphatic one, like a train alongside a mounted bandit. And who is that masked man? The first person singular.

A word on the title, and the divisions beneath it. Sky = air = *Fresh Air*, that pristine radio venue, oral vaudeville, my broadcasting floor of Bakelite. Train = a series of discreet units joined together. It consists of seven sections: Engine drives the collection with pieces that are nearest the places in me where the stories come from; Firebox contains the stories that swirl around Fort York in downtown Toronto; Countryside takes us outside, to Manitoba, France, and the Royal Botanical Gardens; Couplings holds the romances; Sleepers is full of stories I don't know what else to do with; Grand Central Station is the terminus for tales that wind up in New York City; and, lastly, Steam gouts out stories that go P-kshh! The Notes at the back give the broadcast dates and ancillary information, when necessary. References such as "last spring" or "a few weeks ago" have been retained to preserve the air of immediacy these pieces had when delivered. Arcane spellings, punctuation, and grammatical constructions, when they occur, are my responsibility entirely.

The stories to come bear witness to many blessings. They are for whomever believes one's own experiences are a worthy lens through which to focus the world — be that world great or small, lost or present (I can't really tell the difference anymore). Thank you for reading them.

Arcadia, Toronto
Spring, 2001

15

ENGINE

Moving the Bathurst Street Bridge in 1931.

Wade in the Water

Picture this: at night, in a snowstorm, on the waters just southeast of Toronto Island, a schooner bearing a load of cordwood lies wrecked in a gale. No one even knows she's there until the following morning, when Island fishermen find bits of the ship's cargo washed up on the beach. Her crew, barely visible in the white-out, cling to her shrouds and pray.

On shore, two men strip down to their Victorian underwear and spring into a skiff; fishermen wade into the water to push them off. Breakers upset the little boat three times before it reaches the schooner, where one man leaps aboard to lead the crew to safety. He cannot: they are frozen to the ship, "iced up six inches thick" by the hoary spray, the freezing waves nailing them where they've waited so long. Taking a piece of cordwood from the broken hold, the rescuer proceeds to pound the ice off the mariners.

It takes seven hours, and seven trips, on this 7th of December, 1868, but the entire crew of the wrecked schooner are ferried ashore. Between trips, the two lifesavers run up and down barefoot in the snow to regain their circulation. One of these men is William Ward, fisherman, constable, gardener, lifesaver. He lived on the eastern end of Toronto Island and left such an imprint in its sands that that portion of it has been called Ward's Island ever since.

One afternoon this summer past, I was wrapping up at work when Bill Freeman, one of our authors, came by. He told me there was a play being put on that evening by the people who live on Ward's Island. I thought, hell, what else am I going to do, go home and watch my pet turtle bite his ceramic frog? On the ferry trip over, Bill, the smile in his face glowing like a harvest moon, explained further.

"Ward, this is a very 'Island' thing; the local kids are all involved, there's a klezmer band, and the play is processional — we're going to follow the actors all over the island."

And so we did. The play, called *Rite of Passage*, began with a flock of angels on stilts carrying paper lanterns on sticks — these were the local children. As they led us to the first stage, we passed a sailor, white-faced, hanging from a lifesaving ladder hooked to the bough of a weeping willow. He seemed to be perpetually in the act of hauling himself from the water and moaned, repeatedly, "Phoebe!"

Stage succeeded stage as we proceeded from place to place, each vignette representing a passage of life: marriage, birth, adolescence. The moon had risen by the time we reached a shadow puppet show put on in a clearing. Here cutout figures, illuminated from behind onto a white screen, enacted the life of William Ward.

When he was fifteen, William took his five sisters boating on Toronto Bay. His father warned him that the wind was too high but William waved him off; he'd been sailing for most of his brief life. After an hour on the water, William brought the boat around, and, in his own words:

"The wind caught the sail and I slipped off the stern ... the boat then filled and capsized, throwing us all into the water. My sisters all rushed toward me ... I righted the boat and got three of the girls out of the water. They all died in the boat. One of the others got into the boat ... and the remaining one held on by the gunwale. The sail again filled, capsizing the boat a second time. Phoebe hung on by the side of the boat as long as she could and then went down."

All the girls, aged five to twelve, were lost. William was rescued by a man who saw the catastrophe and grabbed a boat from the shore. Phoebe was eleven.

After the shadow story, we heard the ghost actor cry in the distance, "Phoebe!" And then, "Save me!"

That was the origin of William Ward, Island lifesaver, who devoted the rest of his life to plucking luckless mariners from Ontario's inland sea; who leapt beneath the curling tops of fourteen-foot breakers to secure lifelines to vessels run aground; who once fistfought by the light of signal fires to convince a crew to brave the waves. He died in 1912, this fisher of men, the "Laird of Ward's Island," with 164 saved souls to his credit. The papers ran a photo on the day he passed which showed a face worn by water, with a stare that had seen the moon at midnight.

Bill and I were close to seeing that too by the time the play's final act took place, on the beach not far from where Ward had kept his life-saving station. A signal fire blazed. Five angel children, their lanterns lit, ditched their stilts and, to the sound of a single fiddle, waded into the water. Rowing slowly in to meet them was a slumped figure in a dory. When they met, the angels got into the boat, one by one. Then the figure rowed the dory out into the lake, bearing its precious cargo, their illuminated lanterns bunching from the boat like a bouquet. The play was done, and landlubbers like me headed for the ferry dock and home. Bill stayed on the Island, where he lives.

Last Saturday, it was warm, and in order to begin this story, I went back to that beach, where the ghost of William Ward had rowed his angel sisters away. I hauled myself onto the life-saving platform, cracked open my notebook in the autumn sun, and remembered how they had seemed to walk on water for him, those children. And I thought about white-faced William, running barefoot in the snow of his lifelong grief, to save, to save. His sisters had become his anchors, held by and holding onto their brother's little boat, until finally, when it could bear no more, they weighed him up to heaven.

Bathurst Street Bridge

D o you know the Bathurst Street Bridge, the one that starts at Front Street and spans the railways that run toward Union Station? Its iron superstructure, painted black, makes a cat's cradle of columns, beams, and girders, with buttonheads on its rivets so huge you'd think, walking over it, you were pacing the deck of a dreadnought.

Part of the bridge dates from 1916, although part of *that* had been built in 1903 and brought from spanning the Humber River. Much reinforced, the 1916 bridge angled southwest from the intersection of Bathurst and Front toward a new streetcar line that chopped off the north wall of Fort York. Then, in 1931, the city decided to straighten Bathurst toward the new industrial landfill south of Fleet Street, near where the Tip Top Tailors building now stands. Using a deadman and tackle, they inched the old section of the bridge along rails laid for the purpose, with the bridge's supports on wooden blocks. A south section was concurrently built to meet up with the redirected north one, and that's the way the bridge has stood ever since, leading straight down to the waterfront. When streetcars roll over it, they sound like great metal birds screeching through the middle of a thundercloud.

I remember that sound especially from when the streetkids' theatre troupe, Die in Debt, put on a production of *Romeo and Juliet* beneath the bridge a few years ago. Viewed from underneath, the bridge's concrete-cased supports form a receding vault of arches, which was appropriate to the play, since both Romeo and Juliet die in a tomb. At first, the actors stopped whatever they were doing when a streetcar roared overhead, but it didn't take long for them to integrate those sounds into the action itself — Juliet's nurse threw up her arms in resignation and rolled her eyes, for example, as if Renaissance Verona were being casually blitzed with industrial noise.

Later, one winter evening, I was walking home across the bridge when I saw a train that seemed to be on fire from its undersides, creeping toward Bathurst Street from the Parkdale yards in the west. As it slowly ground along, without a window lit or passenger visible, the spitting fire was revealed to be a constant wave of sparks cascading outward from the wheels, about fifteen feet to either side of the engine and its five demonic cars. What I didn't know at the time was that, with continued traffic, the surface of railways spreads out. This puts pressure on the flanged wheels of trains, and can force them off the tracks. Grinding the rails back to their original dimensions is cheaper than replacing them outright, and that's what this service train was doing. After it passed, the snow on either side was either gone, or black. The train itself seemed abandoned; as I said, you couldn't see a soul on board, as if it had been traversing all of North America, on its own, since the Last Spike.

As you climb the bridge from the south side, walking away from the water, Historic Fort York appears on the left, where

Toronto started in 1793. You have to imagine the fort, in its late Georgian heyday, almost entirely surrounded by water, with Lake Ontario lapping its south face, and the marsh of Garrison Creek tufting its northeast side, bullrushed and birded where now there's only the creak of steel. That's where the Grand Trunk put in its railway corridor, replacing frog-song with freight trains.

Bridges are nowhere, always spanning disparate places, themselves placeless, suspended. To stand on the Bathurst Street Bridge after a rain, smelling the wet concrete first poured into its flanking sidewalks in 1916, caught up with looking at its top-chorded columns, cross-stitched with metal bars, makes a place amid the transit, rumbling across and below it, like stopping in a stream. Once, walking south across the bridge to get to Fort York, I found five brightly coloured plastic raspberries clustered together on one of its broad iron shoulders, as if it had borne fruit overnight. False fruit from a no place, but also, I thought, a gift, wrought from something that has borne so much of the city, beside it, below it, above.

Summer Stars

Late Sunday night on the Labour Day weekend, my friend Adam Lynde and I were wandering around in a golf course in Niagara-on-the-Lake. The only light came from a crescent moon and the end of Adam's cigar. We were looking for Fort Mississauga.

"Come on, history boy," I called out, before bumping into a tree. Adam is a doctor of military history who works dispatch for a trucking company in Bolton. It's not often he gets to visit his chosen field.

Somewhere in the moonlit landscape, amidst sand traps and putting greens, lay a star fortification from the tail end of the War of 1812. Adam and I stumbled on, prying the darkness for sunken bastions and a central tower.

It has been a summer of fortifications. The first was Fort Henry, the citadel of Upper Canada. Through the winter, I had edited their new guidebook: an illustrated history with a line of scarlet soldiers across the cover, giving the browser the eyes left.

To celebrate the book's release, Ron Ridley, the curator of Fort Henry, invited me to see one of their sunset ceremonies. So, on a Wednesday afternoon, I knocked off work early, and drove with a friend from Toronto to Kingston.

I had last seen this ceremony a quarter of a century ago. During our cross-continental camping trips of the seventies, my parents took me to the fort, a limestone redoubt arrowing into Lake Ontario, where I was smit with its seemingly cybernetic drill squad. The loudspeaker commentary sounded like an out-take from *The Ten Commandments*. The miracle of Fort Henry's preservation, and the providence of my parents then, were one. The strong bones of my mother echoed in the limestone of the fort's ramparts and casemates.

I can still see the former Fort Henry Guard emerging from their dark portal onto the floodlit parade square; I can hear the hammers of their hobnails striking the anvil of the asphalt. They were all male, all white, all over six feet tall. They were completely contained, and expressed themselves only by explosions — the beat of their drums, the blast of their guns, their controlled shouts to wake the dead. All these sounds reverberated and crashed back at them within the stone polygon of the parade: a hard, angled chamber containing hard, angled men. I thought, then: This must be the spirit incarnadine of what preserved our impossible border.

This time, two things were very different. First, ads for sponsors were thrown in with the commentary, since Canadians no longer believe their historic sites should be adequately funded. Second, there are women in the Fort Henry Guard. This should come as no surprise to anyone, but it hit me like a martial drag show. And yet the obvious objection — that there were no women in the line in Queen Victoria's army — melted in the sounds of female NCOs belting out orders, brandishing sabres, training artillery on the invisible foe. To see a female form go by, swinging a Snider Enfield to that staccato tap of hobnails, was frankly ravishing.

So the Fort Henry Guard no longer presents a six-foot-tall wall of men. I asked Ron if he thought the irregular heights in the guard now make it appear much more like your typical cross-section of nineteenth-century infantry. He did. Ron loves his job, and it's mutual: the respect he was shown that evening by staff as they passed him wasn't just due to his wearing a jet-black, braided, officer's uniform. That night, I left Fort Henry wondering at how present change can bring us closer to fixed history.

Adam and I were having a hard time getting a fix on anything in that crazy golf course. Then a vague shape, darker than the dark sky, rose low before us. It was one of Fort Mississauga's pointy bastions, rounded by the lapse of time, sloping into a ditch that embraced the entire sunken star. Adam circled the ditch until he found a bridge of earth leading to the open gate, called to me, and then we waltzed right in.

Star fortifications were born of the dream that shaped earth could serve our geometries. The dream came true because earthworks are stronger than stone when it comes to stopping cannon-balls: like martial artists, they absorb the impact, or deflect the shot along their stellar angles. They cover themselves with crownworks, counterguards, and lunettes. To come upon one of these in the middle of a golf course at night, illumined by a sliver of moon, is like landing on another planet without leaving mother earth. Fort Mississauga, swaddled in grass, with a central tower soaring like a medieval keep, stands, open and uninterpreted, dumb counterpoise to everything around it.

Adam and I walked and stopped, stood and stared. We whispered so as not to be heard; shouted to be not afraid. We peered into sally ports that lead from the fort's inner ward to the outer world like masonry'd keyholes. I wondered, if I walked through one of them, beneath the soft arm of earth thrown up against the invader, what brave new world I'd find on the other side. Fort Mississauga, untouched from its time, changes anyway, rounding and sprouting. Fort Henry, fixed in stone, changes too, through the flux of bodies that animate it now.

At the end of each sunset ceremony, the Fort Henry Guard form up at the far end of the parade square and sing the soldier's hymn:

> Abide with me —
> Fast falls the eventide.
> The darkness deepens;
> Lord with me abide.
> When other helpers fail
> And comforts flee,
> Help of the helpless,
> O, abide with me.

And then the lights go out, and then we're left alone, in a soaring stone redoubt beneath the stars.

Mercer Union

There was a shirt sale held in Toronto's garment district just before Christmas. A merchant commandeered two floors deep inside the large loft building at the southwest corner of King and Spadina: second floor for men's, sixth for women's. On the men's floor he installed a fake security guard — the clothes alone made that man — and on folding tables laid out samples for twenty bucks and under. All his inventory was stored beneath each table, in boxes. A large, handmade, cardboard sign in day-glo colours announced the sale, just beside one of the entry doors that gives onto King.

I like that door. It also leads into Mercer Union, a small artist-run gallery. Some time before the shirt sale, I walked into Mercer Union for the first time and found an installation by Michael Fernandez entitled "I am a failure": You enter a space in the middle of which sits a child-sized table and chair. The surrounding walls are ruled, like an elementary speller, from top to bottom. And the phrase "I am afraid of ..." crams each and every inch and line, written down by hand, with an almost infinite variation of endings. I asked the person at the front desk about the origin of those, and she told me that, as the installation was going up, visitors were encouraged to write their fears out on sheets, which were kept by the artist; these, along with the artist's own fears, were then transcribed on the walls. At the exit end of the room was a large red arrow, pointing out.

Now, at first I thought, Oh no, the Installation from Hell — I'll follow that arrow out the door, and never go to another gallery again. But then I thought: Maybe there's something here for you. So I stood and spot-read in this classroom of litanized fears, and identified and laughed a little and wondered: How can so many of these be mine? Then I put together various dramatic possibilities that the installation suggested, one of which was: You're kept after school for being afraid. You know, how the teacher punishes you by having you write "I will not, dot dot dot"? Only in this case, the student had written, not what she would not do, but what she does: *fears* — and so had written those out, and was allowed to leave school, to go and play in the world.

As it turns out, Mercer Union is called Mercer Union because it's run by an artists' co-operative, and used to be housed on nearby Mercer Street. At the time, however, I thought it was named after the mercers — an old term for textile merchants — located in Toronto's garment district, such as the guy who ran the shirt sale. At the end of each working day, the remaining sweatshops around lower Spadina Avenue give a small, manufacturing shrug, leaving snipped bits of multi-coloured material stashed into clear plastic sacks, like rainbows contained; or curbside fabric cascades, bunching out of cardboard boxes held together by ribbons of ripped cloth.

Now this is the strange part. If you lift the street-dusty carpet that lies just inside the door that leads to Mercer Union, you'll see the words "The Samuel Building" mosaic'd into the floor. It's a rough job, swamped by the carpet, but otherwise as permanent as a Byzantine billboard. I've tried to find out who exactly Samuel was, without certain success; he could have been the owner. But it's not so much the who but the where of the title that sets Samuel apart from his neighbours.

The other loft buildings in the neighbourhood, the exultant Balfour, the humble Krangle, the gothic Commodore, the rooked Darling, the sober Reading, even the disfigured, dignified Weld, display their names proudly, incised or in relief in stone. Samuel keeps his name to himself. Maybe he doesn't have to advertise; after all, isn't it common knowledge that Jewish Torontonians made the garment district what it was? And was not Samuel a mighty, if somewhat misguided, prophet in Israel? The bold, deco Balfour Building would agree, named as it is, by architect Benjamin Brown, after the Earl of Balfour, who championed the idea of the state of Israel as early as 1917. But maybe Samuel, which means "heard by God," knows he doesn't have to shout so loud, guarding a door that leads into fresh garments and out of fear.

Rock of Ages

I was sweeping up in some halfway house the other night and taking the dustpan to the garbage beneath the sink, and there sat Northrop Frye, bent over a book at the kitchen table. So this was where he wound up after all those years of teaching the bible and literature! I started cleaning the kitchen and began humming "Rock of Ages" to pass the time when, wouldn't you know it, Dr. Frye joined in with the words "Rock of ages, cleft for me, Let me hide myself in thee" except, instead of singing the next line "Let the water and the blood," he sang "Let the glory and the flood." Wasn't that just like him, I thought, as I scrubbed the countertop, to introduce metaphoric equivalents even here! We finished the hymn together in a long, drawn-out harmony, like a barbershop duet, and then looked at each other. I couldn't stop smiling, even in the dream, and said, "That was beautiful."

"Yes," Dr. Frye said, like the kindly, understated man he was, "that was very nice."

For most of the second half of the twentieth century, Northrop Frye taught at Victoria College in Toronto. He was Canada's foremost literary critic, and yet I always found that epithet bookish and — worse — peevish when applied to him. The titles of his own works — *Fearful Symmetry, Anatomy of Criticism, The Great Code* — sound like trumpets. When he lectured, his gravely, periodic voice didn't belong to a critic — you heard the heart and fire of literature itself. Then something bigger than us all would swallow the classroom, drawing in Frye's draughts of words, and, like Jonah's whale, carry us through a literal sea.

Our great teacher has been gone for ten years now. The winter he died, I got a call from Jim Carscallen, a colleague of Frye's, who asked me if I would fly up from New Jersey to speak on behalf of the student body at the memorial service. At the time, I was on a scholarship at the graduate English department of Rutgers University, a privilege I enjoyed by virtue of Frye's letter of reference. I said yes, of course, I would be honoured. The honour of my life. I flew to the tiny Island airport, just south of where I now live, crossed the narrow Western Gap by ferry, and trundled north on a streetcar to the University of Toronto.

When I arrived, Convocation Hall was packed. All I remember now is that when Bob Rae got up to speak, he went on forever, but Margaret Atwood was funny. She was really funny. She told how, talking to Frye, he would address his reply to your shoes. Afterwards, I turned to her.

"I liked what you said," I said.

"Thank you," she replied. "I liked what you said too."

The service over, I headed for Chinatown, cold and famished. I turned down Spadina and ran smack into Moy Lin-Shin, the tai chi master who had sponsored me at school the two years prior to my taking Frye's bible course. When I had no money for rent, Moy let me stay in the Taoist temple on D'Arcy Street for an entire winter. This winter night, he asked me if I wanted to come to supper. I said I was meeting friends, which was true, but I was sorry not to have accepted. Master Moy had helped keep me warm, well fed, and healthy during my feckless years as an undergraduate.

He also taught me how to move, so I was always fascinated to watch Dr. Frye's gestures in the classroom. Standing behind his lectern, he would take two steps forward, two back, raise his hand as if he were swearing on the bible, and then, for emphasis, frame space with his open palms. This academic two-step would go on for fifty minutes while the man spoke, pause by pause, his *sententiae* clear water from a rock. Indeed, his lectures felt so fresh you would think he coined them on the spot, so I was always amazed, afterwards, reading on the train home, to find them embedded word for word in *The Great Code*. Frye practiced perpetual spontaneity.

One way he read the Christian bible was through typology. So, for example, the serpent which Moses makes out of brass, and raises on a pole to heal the Israelites bitten by real snakes in the wilderness, becomes a *type* of Christ, lifted up on the cross, who saves us from the infernal serpent. The Old and New Testaments thus form a double mirror, between which their myriad characters and figures — foretold in the Old, fulfilled in the New — are infinitely reflected. And yet, for all its zap and power, sometimes this divine funhouse of reading left me gasping for irreducible particulars.

The paper I wrote for the course — the one which secured Dr. Frye's recommendation for grad school — came out of that desert. "Let us look at a group of female figures in the bible," Frye writes in *The Great Code*, and so I did. "This essay runs on the belief that the stories in the Old Testament are significant in and of themselves," my notes ingenuously proclaimed, "and further that the way they are told, even in translation — that is to say the texture of the narrative, the feel of the story as it moves through the King's English — is also part of their meaning now."

There was nothing new in my approach, but bear in mind I was an undergraduate, and smart enough to prize my naivety. Still, I was a little lost as to how to proceed. Margaret Burgess, Frye's other half in class, urged me to lose myself in order to find myself in my essay. So I found writing space in a basement room at Emmanuel College, the United Church side of Vic, its Methodist roots showing in every vine that clasps its gothic walls. I would leave my papers, my King James Bible, and my Concordance unguarded when I went for coffee or to classes, consulted no external sources, and relied on the pages of the Authorized Version to open where I needed them. Well-met Rebekah, promised Rachel, Rahab and plaintive Ruth took all my love, as I watched their stories shift and differ.

When Rebekah filled her pitcher, fulfilling prophecy at the same time, she watered my desert of grandiose visions; when Jacob rolled the stone from the well, kissed Rachel, and lifted up his voice and wept, I felt a rock had been rolled from the cave of typology.

And yet, Frye's spirit appeared everywhere I read, a pillar of cloud and fire, both vague and particular, going before, leading a great procession of figures to each their own destination. When, a year later, Northrop lead us physically at the Victoria graduation service, I saw his flowing purple robes for what they were: a majestic excuse to bring us to holy ground — the glory of education, and the flood of stories that we tell and retell in the halfway house of earth.

FIREBOX

Michael at Historic Fort York in the summer of 1983.

Impurvious

Ken Purvis is chief interpreter at Historic Fort York, that embanked triangle of turf just west from downtown Toronto. Recently, before winter scarfed the fort's eight remaining buildings in snow, he took me on an informal tour of the grounds. In particular, I was curious about the newly clad and whitewashed blockhouses. You can see them as you drive by the fort from the Bathurst Street Bridge: rectangular, two-storey wooden buildings that have calmly braved the elements here since 1813. They are the oldest structures, still in use, in the city.

Ken is casually encyclopedic about the fort's heritage. He started working for the Toronto Historical Board just as I was on my way out, sometime back in the hoary 1980s. At that time, he was fresh from fifing and marching at Canada's historical Hollywood, Old Fort Henry, in Kingston. There was — supposedly — this big rivalry between the staff at Fort York and the Fort Henry Guard: a rivalry of which, Ken later told us, the animators at Fort Henry remain totally unaware. Fort Henry bulks above Kingston in solid limestone, and the drill-precision of its guard makes the nineteenth-century dream of industrial infantry come true. Historic Fort York is surrounded with sod and almost run over by the Gardiner Expressway. If you go there, you learn about the past.

When I worked at the fort, those two ancient blockhouses were dark to look at: dark like the old-growth trees they carry the memory of in their timbers, two-eyed on every side with paned windows cut, somewhat bombastically, for cannon. Blockhouse No. 2, the bigger one in the centre of the fort, was always the scariest building to lock up for the night. I had to shut off the internal lighting while far from the exit door and then feel my way out, around the little Theatre of War housed on the lower level, its diorama fretted with Christmas lights to indicate troop movements: red, blue; red, blue. When I lifted the heavy lock leading out, it was always with a sigh of relief: another day of duty, done; another dodge of bogus ghosts, down.

Ken's impromptu tour was studded with stories about how artifacts had come to light during recent excavations and renovations. While we were in the second storey of that central blockhouse, he reached up to one of the horizontal ceiling beams and said, "Guess what we found here?" I blinked, wide-eyed. A brass belt plate? A soldier's diary? "A button stick," Ken announced triumphantly, with a mischievous glint in his eyes.

You see, the soldiers had to shine their buttons, but not the uniforms the buttons were attached to, so they placed these slotted sticks between button and cloth to protect their clothes from polish. Now, during the War of 1812, the blockhouses were full of bunk beds; someone who slept on the top must have used that ceiling beam as an informal shelf for his stuff. When I asked Ken how old he thought the stick was, he dated it to during or just after the war itself. Whether that soldier's regiment was moved, or he died, or just forgot about it, that stick remained stashed away for almost two hundred years. "I love stories like that," Ken said.

Back outside, we admired the clean lines and white sheen of the blockhouse, and I asked Ken the reason for the change. When the fort was restored in the 1930s, they took off the clapboards that barked the blockhouses in the mistaken belief that they hadn't been there in 1813. The result was that the fort ended up resembling a frontier outpost, rather than an urbane military hotel, as the Georgians preferred. In a way, I thought, the restorers had been right: since Toronto has burgeoned around it, Fort York has remained an outpost, lost for over a century in the city's own forest of smokestacks, gasworks, slaughterhouses, and freight. The demise of indigenous manufacturing has reduced the city's over-storey in its turn, while a new curatorial vision at the fort led to its blockhouses being clad and whitewashed again, as they were in the beginning.

The British Army left Canada in the 1870s. While we know a fair amount about its officers, we know less about the underclass they commanded. The ordinary infantrymen's lives are as buried as they are, from the battlefields of Niagara to their forgotten graveyard, paved over under Wellington Street. But Ken has captured one of their casual gestures at least, just by reaching up, to help shine the image of Canada's vanished soldiery.

Green Tigers

My friend Barrie and I cycled through the Niagara Peninsula one summer not too long ago. Starting from Burlington, we jumped the escarpment at Ancaster and headed for the Grand River, just opposite the Six Nations Reserve. From there, we wound our way past cornfields and through the towns of Caledonia, Cayuga, and Dunnville, hugging the river on our right, until we came to Port Maitland on Lake Erie. From there, almost incoherent from fatigue, we crawled along the Erie shore into Port Colborne and collapsed at the Capri Motel, somewhere north on what felt like the outskirts of town. That was the first day. We were so tired, I felt more like we were on the outskirts of reality.

Earlier, we'd stopped in a donut shop in Dunnville, trying to fortify ourselves before the last leg to Port Colborne.

"A lemonade prease," I said to the bemused young woman behind the counter.

Then it was Barrie's turn. He was fishing for some change, so I asked him, "Do you need a penny?"

"Yes," he replied, "do you have one?"

I stared at him a moment. "No," I whined. Why had I even offered? We were pretty far gone.

The next day we came across an old British fort from the War of 1812 so appallingly interpreted that we christened it "Fort Bogatron" for the amount of bogusness that went on inside it. There, we were told by one tour guide that the soldiers stood out in the cold and died of "penewmonia." I'm not sure why everyone seemed to be mispronouncing things on this trip. We were also informed that the drummer boys were all shot in battle because they were used as little shields by the men. Leaving Fort Bogatron in the mists of its time, we headed up to Niagara Falls, where we were visually assaulted by a sign-studded bonanza of cheap hotels, each equipped with poolside furniture that made me think I was about to "Meet George Jetson!" That second day was hell. It's also when the tendonitis I'd achieved in my left ankle began to start up.

Barrie is a hospital pharmacist and an avid cyclist. We met in high school, and used to play war games together in one or another of our parents' basements. We always talked about battles. Barrie was also one of the stars of the football team, and even I got to be class Valedictorian. Our high school years were lucky, that way. Cycling down the Grand River that first day, we passed what looked like a replica of Aldershot, the school we went to in Burlington: same design, but a different location. Horses grazing in surrounding fields where Aldershot would have had parked cars; the river in the distance rather than Highway 2. It was weird, as if our collective past had been picked up and plunked down in a green world somewhere else.

In keeping with that, day three was different. We took the bicycle path that meanders between the Niagara Parkway and the river. Rather than being hounded and pounced on by cars, we now passed trees and grasses, as the path leapt a little to the left or the right, and we rose and fell with its swells as our racers hummed along. Halfway to Niagara-on-the-Lake we came upon MacFarlane House, a loyalist residence that served as a hospital during the War of 1812. Musket-balls have pockmarked its red brick exterior, a rare finish for a Canadian home. Now it's a homespun café. As we sat out on the porch and ate, Barrie and I realized we had finally arrived at the kind of trip we'd set out looking for in the first place: historic, pastoral and, like us, relatively clean-cut.

At Queenston Heights, we went over the battlefield and ended up at the redan battery, near which, on October 13th, 1812, General Sir Isaac Brock was killed. I wanted to find where a single company of the 49th Regiment had stumbled uphill, trying to retake the redan after it fell to the Americans that October day. My tendonitis had me stumbling around as well, but I found what I think was the ground they traversed, overgrown and unmarked. The men of the 49th were called the Green Tigers, from both the colour of their cuffs and the ferocity of their fighting. Their counter-attack, with the doomed Brock at their head, is one of the tiny, futile, outlandish events that pockmark the terrain of 1812 battlefields. It's hard to believe that Canada was once tiny, futile, and outlandish, too ... at least, so it must have seemed to both Loyalists and Yankees alike.

And I thought about that diminutive detachment, those stumbling tigers, who passed there. Canadians pass them now as cars pass cyclists. They have no right of way on our memory lanes. Back on the road, my tendonitis was worse than ever. I should have stopped long before I did, limping back to Niagara-on-the-Lake to phone for a ride home. I should have stopped, bicycles should stay off the highways, and Brock should have waited for the reinforcements that were coming to win the day for him after he was dead. But he didn't wait, I didn't stop at Dunnville, we all continue towards various woundings. I think of Barrie and I, our sinews knit to peddling, pacing and passing each other those three days. The thing is to push forward, until you can't pedal anymore. Reinforcements are coming, as was my ride, to carry the day for us.

Canadian Corps

I went to the Fort York Armouries near the exhibition grounds in Toronto the other night to watch some friends practise military drill. Bruce, Kevin, and Chris belong to the 20th Battalion of the Canadian Expeditionary Force. The C.E.F. is the collective name for the soldiers Canada sent overseas to fight during the First World War. Now, my friends are not time travellers: their present-day 20th Battalion is a commemorative unit only. They went to France a few years back, for example, to mark the 75th anniversary of the 1918 Armistice; they turn up at Remembrance Day parades wearing their sober, khaki uniforms and carrying Lee Enfield rifles.

Outfitted in the same fashion, their originals marched into a war that annihilated drill as a field exercise. They were caught between the Battle of Waterloo, a century earlier, when moving many bodies as one brought victory, and what we know now: a world where weapons so overmatch the fragile humans which handle them that only hiding makes sense. And their arms —

those Lee Enfields — look like lampstand furniture compared to what most soldiers carry today. The young Canadians who drilled at Exhibition Park in 1914, just west of the Fort York Armouries, knew nothing of the machine-gun maw which lay gaping for them in the fields of France.

Speaking of fields, just south of the armouries and along the Lake Ontario shore lies Coronation Park. It sports a small forest, containing maples mainly, planted in 1937 by the Toronto chapter of an international group called Men of the Trees. They planted trees in place of trenches, as if to convert aggression into conservation. In that spirit, Coronation Park became a commemorative arboretum: many a tree has a small brass plaque, greened by time and fixed in stone, flush with the earth at its base.

But the plaques are ciphers — they make sense only to whomever happens to have an order of battle for the Canadian Expeditionary Force at hand. I went out one blowy, overcast afternoon, armed with graphite sticks and sheets of paper, to take rubbings of them, as you might do at a graveyard. I brought my findings home and figured them out with the aid of a military history book. 78th BN., for example, stands for the 78th (Winnipeg Grenadiers) Battalion; 4th TREN.MORT. stands for the 4th Trench Mortar Battery; 2nd BN. M.G.C. stands for the 2nd Battalion, Machine Gun Corps, and so on. The letters C.E.F. conclude each legend in the plaques' shorthand cemetery.

If you're not told those markers are there, it's hard to guess that they exist at the base of each tree. Just so, it's easy to miss how much the ground surrounding them is saturated in military history: the lower west end of Toronto is built on Garrison Common — the land set aside for the army when the city was first founded as the Town of York; the statue of Winged Victory that heralds the entrance to the Canadian National Exhibition extends her garland arm above Toronto's only battlefield from the War of 1812; and just north of the Fort York Armouries and the old fort itself, streets named after the warriors Wellington and Tecumseh quietly define the Niagara neighbourhood.

Old soldiers haunt this corner of Toronto. Follow Niagara Street as it curves along the buried bed of Garrison Creek, past the near-human cries that issue from the pig slaughterhouse on Wellington, and you come upon the statue of a First World War infantryman. He stands at attention, his body canted slightly forward, as was the manner of soldiers a century before him, who leaned into their marching for momentum. He wears a cap, not a helmet, as if he has yet to see the trenches: a green recruit. Up close, however, you may notice his hands, relaxed at his sides. Moreover, he wears webbing like my friends in the 20th Battalion do, from the middle of the war, so it's clear he's faced the blast of battle. And, far from being green — the greened bronze of most war memorials — this veteran is brown: khaki-coloured, the colour of the Canadian infantry he embodies, and of the dirt they tore into, soon enough, for shelter.

The statue stands on a granite slab in front of the last branch of the Canadian Corps Association. The association sprang from a massive reunion of First World War vets held at the exhibition grounds in 1934. Over 100,000 men showed up "to perpetuate the spirit of the old Canadian Corps' front-line soldier," as well as to fight for pensions and medical care for veterans in need. That event inspired the Men of the Trees to name their forest after units from the Canadian Expeditionary Force, of which the Canadian Corps was the primary field element.

Last summer, on the 18th of June, Bruce and I went to the Wheat Sheaf Tavern to mark the 183rd anniversary of the Battle of Waterloo. My old friend was about to drive me home when, without a word, he whipped his car around and drove us to the statue, about two blocks away from the Sheaf. There, we clambered out of the car and fell to admiring the Canadian Corps soldier. Then we noticed something odd: the inscription beneath the statue tells you his monument is recycled. It was donated by the Borden Company, and on the back of the slab — which was once the front — is a list of employees who died in both World Wars. Above those names, two bronze maple leaves, patina'd like the plaques in Coronation Park, lie halfway open. I pressed my palms into them. Those leaves, I now realize, keep faith with the waterfront trees that, each spring, make the statue's memory green. At night, it's illuminated from behind and, as Bruce and I drove away, we saw the shadow the canting figure ghosts forward in deadly earnest.

Back at the Fort York Armouries, the volunteers of the 20th Battalion went through their evolutions, shouldering and porting their arms, fixing and unfixing bayonets, and choreographing an eighty-year-old dance that has not been seen, *en masse*, since 1918. During a break, Bruce, Kevin, and Chris came over to talk. They were sheepish about what they were doing so well. Since we had all worked at Historic Fort York together, years ago, they were worried I would think that they should have left the parade square behind them by now.

Nothing could have been further from my mind. It was a pleasure to see my friends drill again, both distinct and uniform: intimate infantry. Watching them was like seeing the statue on Niagara Street come to life. At the end of their practice, these commemorative soldiers planted their feet in understated attention, retaining the soldier-shape Canada once sent overseas to shake the nations of the earth and, by so doing, became one of them.

Isaac's Ladder

I was talking to a woman named Nathalie at a party the other evening who grew up not far from Crysler's Farm. Crysler's Farm lay along the banks of the St. Lawrence River, between Prescott and Cornwall. One of the most important battles of the War of 1812 was fought there. Nathalie told me that she has stood, more than once, on a particular country lane near the old battlefield during a storm and watched the rain fall on just one-half of the road. "It's weird there," she said.

I visited the battlefield on a camping trip with my family when I was a kid. It was the 1970s — cars were huge and public funding for heritage sites was even huger. Our centre of operations was a campground on the Canadian side of the St. Lawrence. From there, we visited Upper Canada Village, which was right by us, as well as Fort Wellington, in Prescott, and Fort Henry, in Kingston. I was in historic heaven. The best part was that I could walk from our campsite to the Crysler's Farm Visitor Centre and stare at its vast mural of the battle as often as

I wanted. The worst part was that half of the battlefield is under water. It was flooded when the St. Lawrence Seaway was created in the late 1950s.

So it was impossible to traverse the actual ground where, on a wet and overcast November 11th, 1813, lean, meagre lines of British infantry stood in the fields near John Crysler's farm — the 49th Regiment wearing gray greatcoats, echoing the angry sky; the 89th Regiment in brick red, matching the autumn leaves. The Americans came on, a torrent of blue, spilling out of the swampy woods. They faced the primeval geometry of the 89th wheeling to face them. The British muskets went up, then levelled — a row of matchsticks striking the cloud cover. They delivered a series of crashing volleys — fire by wings, then by platoons, rolling their thunder from right to left — that scattered the invaders amongst the tree stumps of the recently cleared fields.

A violent downpour followed the fighting and, in a way, forecast what would happen to the battlefield in the next century. During the overcast days that my family spent camping near Crysler Park, I walked through the tall, wet grass many times. The fact that a complete rainbow would sometimes appear, spanning the American and Canadian sides of the St. Lawrence, did not stop me from imagining lines of British infantry, hurling volleys repeatedly, like a bulkhead door slamming again and again against the blue deluge. The rain-divided road that Nathalie has witnessed reminds me of those soldiers, whose sodden ground, like half our history, has gone under the flood of progress.

This summer, I got a call from my old friend Matt Mcdonald. Matt is a major in the Canadian Armed Forces. He and I worked at Historic Fort York together in Toronto many years ago. Matt is also a ski instructor to the Canadian Army — in other words, he's in pretty fine shape. He suggested that he, his wife, Heather, and I should do some cycling in the Niagara

Peninsula. So, on a weekend, the three of us drove to Niagara-on-the-Lake with our bikes in the back of Matt's van. We parked just outside the town, not far from Fort George, where, in the predawn of October 13th, 1812, Major General Isaac Brock awoke to the sound of artillery pounding his positions downriver at Queenston.

The bicycle path that my friends and I set out on is the most lovely of its kind in Ontario. It also follows the route Brock rode to Queenston Heights. The path ribbons alongside the Niagara River, and is punctuated by historic plaques, Loyalist homes, orchards, and ravines. The ravines make the path rise and fall in felicity to the contours of the land, which is a major part of the pleasure riding it. Isaac Brock must have felt otherwise, as he urged his horse, Alfred, to swallow the ground and bring him to the fighting. Brock's bloodless victory at Detroit had united the province of Upper Canada behind him, but a foolish truce had given the Americans time to regroup. When he dismounted at the village of Queenston, he found them swarming ashore.

Brock's first thought was to order the light company of his own 49th Regiment away from the heights to help their fellow grenadier company in the village. This allowed the Americans to gain the high ground unobserved, and they sent Brock, leading Alfred by the reins, tumbling down to Queenston. There, Isaac rallied the wing companies of his beloved 49th, tethered Alfred to a fence, said "Take breath boys, you will need it in a few moments." They flew back up and down the heights two more times that day. The first attack cost Isaac his life; Alfred was killed in the second, ridden by Brock's aide-de-camp.

At the foot of Queenston Heights, now, is a stone, and a cenotaph, and a statue of a horse in a glass case. Matt, Heather, and I passed them as we took the bicycle path to Brock's monument, a massive pillar cresting the heights. On our way back, I asked my friends to stop so that I could find out what they signified. The horse is Alfred, cast in bronze like the guns toward which he galloped, undercresting his master. Did he say Ha, ha, among the trumpets, like the good book says war horses do, his neck clothed with thunder? Next to him, the small cenotaph, in counterpoint to the exalting pillar above, marks the place where Isaac Brock fell. Lastly, the stone honours the warriors from the Six Nations who contained and terrified the Americans after Isaac and Alfred's deaths until reinforcements arrived, achieving victory and, as with the battle at Crysler's Farm a year later, preserving the Canadas.

When Jacob, the son of the biblical Isaac, awoke from his dream of a ladder spanning heaven and earth, with angels ascending and descending on it, he took the stone he'd used as a pillow and set it up for a pillar. I saw the single stone below, and the pillar above Queenston Heights, and joined Jacob in my heart, saying "How dreadful is this place!" And yet, the name Isaac, translated, means *He will laugh*. I like to think that both horse and rider still do — and mock at fear, too, when they see one battlefield where Canada was preserved, preserved, where the spirits of red-coated infantry descend and ascend, climbing over the autumn leaves.

Mike's Drum

Last spring, I led a walking tour through Garrison Common in downtown Toronto. Garrison Common comprised the lands set aside for the British Army when the city was first settled, in 1793, as the Town of York. Eighty-seven stalwart *Fresh Air* listeners followed Jeff and me as we set out from the military graveyard at Victoria Square, crossed the Bathurst Street Bridge behind Historic Fort York, swept through the memorial forest of Coronation Park, and wound up in front of the old fort itself. After concluding remarks, we passed inside its sloping sod walls for well-earned refreshments.

In the northwest bastion of Fort York, a large canvas marquee is raised each spring for guests. There Ken Purvis, a friend and former colleague, was waiting for us. He had laid out chairs and tables and stood beaming behind a makeshift bar as we entered the vast tent. In military fashion, he had placed a rope-tension snare drum on the centre table. He had also set the appetizers around the drum, so that people would draw near to its wooden shell painted with regimental arms, its calfskin heads and catgut snares, all bound together by heavy ropes that zigzag'd round its body like the iron trusses on the Bathurst Street Bridge.

I was touched by Ken's attention to detail and went over to thank him.

"Do you know whose drum that is?" Ken asked in his melodious baritone.

"No," I said, a bit taken aback that it was anybody's in particular.

"That's Mike's drum," Ken answered. "I thought you'd appreciate it."

I did. Back in the early 1980s, when I worked at the fort, Mike was the ensign of us all. In the bizarre but colourful world of historical re-enactment, Michael was a little Mars, a god of war. His slightest movements, his every phrase, were cause for emulation. "Listen up, you bone-idle crows," he would say, regaling a group of us on the parade ground, who were in turn bursting through the whitewashed crosses on our scarlet wool uniforms to be more like him. He spoke in a self-made patois of field-exercise English and contemporary slang. He explained nineteenth-century military drill as if it were ballet, and he performed it, in his twenty-third year, like an old master.

Before Fort York became the respectable museum it is today, the Fort York Guard were rented out at various venues in Toronto like the city's own red-coated chorus line. But Michael did something else. While we fired our muskets above jubilant meeting planners, opened Canada's Wonderland with a bang, or shot field artillery to celebrate multiculturalism, he raised entire units of volunteer re-enactors to do the authentic thing. I'll never forget the day he brought a light infantry platoon he had trained from Fort Wellington in Prescott for us to see: they skimmed over the garrison's grass like a flight of Canada Geese. He formed our first decent fife and drum corps and ordered a drum major's mace from England with which to lead it. Accompanied by the corps' shrill thunder, Michael put the history back into Historic Fort York.

I live near the fort. I've never really left it. I do other things now, but the sight of Fort York, with its sober brick barracks, whitewashed blockhouses, and green-shouldered walls, always takes my breath away. Not long after Michael died, I took to working the night shift there, guarding sleepover school groups with a big black dog called Charlie. It was dark. Even the moony Hyundai sign along with the other billboards that circle the fort like glowing wolves couldn't flush the spooks from my soul as I walked the walls at three a.m. with Charlie close behind. I used to think he romped with the spirits those nights when he bolted behind the barracks in search of new smells. You see, a lot of people perished on Garrison Common: British soldiers, American soldiers, and Michael.

Much more recently, I dreamt about him — one of those dreams that seems to go on forever. We sat together in a small room on the top floor of the Centre Blockhouse. In life, Michael had been larger than life, "too big for the world," as one friend noted. Now, he was subdued. I told him about my writing, and said, "If I'm not published in five years, and living by my pen in ten, you can consider my time here a failed experiment." Michael smiled knowingly. It was such a *Ward* thing to say. He then told me there was a rifle he was looking to buy. He'd seen a lot of them, but there was one in particular he had his eye on. We talked of many other things until daybreak.

I woke up feeling better than I had in years, and went out. It was early fall, and the school programs at the fort were in full swing. As I crossed the Bathurst Street Bridge, I looked into the green field of the fort's parade square and saw a flock of kids tumbling after an interpreter in a scarlet coat. Not such a bad place to be, I said to myself. Maybe the kids keep him company.

From that moment, Michael, who had taken his own life in the Centre Blockhouse, ceased to be the ghost of Garrison Common, and became the genius of the fort — its local protective deity. On the day of the walking tour, Ken had turned Mike's rattling drum into a silent shrine.

Long ago, when soldiers prayed in the field, they would stack their drums into makeshift altars and hold what were called drumhead services. I had not thought of the walking tour as a religious procession, winding towards a tent that would double as a temple. A few days after the event, I spoke to Tom Allen, the former host of *Fresh Air*, and he said, "You know, Ward, radio is about the flesh made word, but your tour was about the word made flesh." Not a bad conclusion to a day that took the sounding shell of memory, and drummed it up again.

COUNTRYSIDE

Paul shows me how high he can lift a bale of hay in the Haute Marne, 1997.

Foulard Romance

In 1985 I spent a summer working on a farm in the Haute
Marne, a hilly, heavily wooded region in France located east
of Paris and south of the Ardennes. It was a dairy farm, run by a
hard-working family, les Bournots, in a town of about two hundred people called Genevrières. Paul, the father, needed someone to help his son, Didier, and himself in the fields. His wife,
Geneviève, occupied herself with the cows, as did, to varying
degrees, their three daughters, Isabel, Catherine, and Véronique.

My placement on the farm was co-ordinated by an agency in
Paris that arranged agricultural exchanges between France and
Québec. I'm not a Quebecer, but Paul was open to anyone who
was willing to work and studying French. I was both: being con-
fined to my course at the Sorbonne winter and spring had made
me desperate for physical labour. A farm seemed as good a place
as any to combine my studies and my body, although I had
never worked on one before, let alone in another language. But
I was prepared in one aspect: I brought with me a handkerchief,

un foulard, black with a paisley white pattern, to wipe away the sweat of my brow.

That summer, this foulard of mine went with me wherever I worked, and was remarked on by the family: sometimes wrapped around my head, like a Canadian kamikaze, as we pitched bales of hay into the loft; other times pouffing out of my pant pockets, as Didier and I trailed after Paul in his tractor in the fields, gathering those bales with pitchforks and quickly calloused palms. It became my talisman until, near the end of *le deuxième coup*, or final harvest, it became lost in the loft, buried somewhere beneath sweet-smelling, Haute Marne hay.

That fall I came back to Canada and began my undergraduate education at the University of Toronto. But Paul, in addition to the myriad of chores the farm tasked him with, was on the lookout for that hankie. Later that winter, a package arrived from Genevrières: it was mon foulard, uncovered while hauling down bales for the cows to eat. Happily, Paul added in the accompanying letter — and I could just hear him laughing — it had not passed through the belly of a cow!

Last summer I returned to the farm at Genevrières for the first time in twelve years. Since my time there, all of Paul's daughters have become nurses, and two of them are married. Didier himself also works in a hospital, and the farm was about to be sold, as Paul and Geneviève headed for a well-earned retirement. When Véronique and her husband, Emmanuel, dropped me off at Paul's front door, he let out a shout of greeting from inside the garage and, from that moment, it felt like I had been gone about two weeks.

Now, it really did feel like I had been gone two weeks, because after we got past the *ça va*s, almost everyone asked: Do you still have that foulard? The one that was lost in the hay? And with what pride did I slowly extract it from my travelling sack! And that first evening back, Paul threw me in the car and we went off, up and down the hills that surround his farm, to see the land, my foulard in my pocket as before.

The next day, the Bournot kids took me to Langres, where most of them now live and work. Langres is an intact, walled hill-town, dating back to Celtic times, fortified by the Romans and then the French. Denis Diderot, the famous encyclopedist, came from its collège. It was also home to Jeanne Mance, one of Canada's first nurses. Baptized at Langres in 1606, she came to New France in 1641 with the express intent of setting up a hospital at Ville-Marie, which is now the island of Montréal. She founded the Hôtel-Dieu hospital there in 1642.

After walking the wide ramparts and narrow ways of Langres with Véronique and Emmanuel, Didier and Catherine, we came to the Place Henriot where, next to a small gazebo and before the cathedral, the statue of Jeanne Mance stands. It was executed by Cardot in 1968 and is simple and unassuming. Jeanne looks off to the left, her arms free at her sides ... with bird-droppings on one of them? True enough, there was a paisley white splotch on her black right forearm. Fortunately, there was also a small fountain by the gazebo, and I knew what to do. Issuing the foulard from my travelling sack, I soaked it in the healing waters of Langres and washed Jeanne's arm clean.

"Oh, you must be photographed with Jeanne Mance!" Paul's nurse-daughters cried after my act of faux-gallantry. I stood beside her. "Take her hand, take her hand!" they exclaimed. As I said, the statue is not imposing, but somehow I didn't think I had the right. It's all well and good to hang out with present-day nurses from Langres, I thought, but to take liberties with Jeanne Mance herself? "Je n'ai pas le droit!" I shouted back.

So there I stand, hands behind my back, in the photo Catherine took while I stood with my little sack carrying the ancient, saved, not-eaten-by-a-cow foulard, which returned to the farm, as I did, twelve years after, and went from wiping the sweat from my brow to bathing Jeanne Mance's arm, that first nurse in an extended family of nurses that took me in, as Canada and its old countries loop back and touch one another.

The Cows Come Home

The other day my mother called my Great Aunt Mae, who's eighty-eight now, and just back on her feet, having fallen and fractured her hip some months ago. Mom is a Winnipegger, but her parents grew up in Carman, Manitoba, a few miles from the small farming community of Roland, where Aunt Mae lives now. She married my mother's Uncle Fred in 1958.

"I can't talk to you right now, Helen Jean," Mae said over the phone, "I'm looking after Ross's cattle — you call Ross instead." My mother assumed Aunt Mae couldn't be serious, although she's not given to joking much these days, so Mom repeated, "I'll be talking to Ross later, Aunt Mae, but just now I'd like to speak with you." But Aunt Mae reiterated: "Helen Jean, I don't have the time right now; I'm looking after Ross's cattle and I'll talk to you later. Good-bye."

My mother thought for a moment, and then did call Ross, her cousin. Ross was raised on a farm not far from Uncle Fred's, but as a young man he first pursued a very successful career with the Royal Bank. When he returned to the land, my Great Uncle Fred took Ross under his wing, as if he were his own son.

It was Ross's wife, Donna, who answered. "I was just talking to Aunt Mae," Mom said, "and she told me she was too busy taking care of Ross's cattle to have much of a conversation." Mom later told me that Donna laughed so hard at this she figured you could hear it all the way to Winnipeg. Then Donna put Ross on the phone.

My Great Uncle Fred was born in Carman 1901. He never took a drink and he never smoked. He lived as sharp as a tack and as strong as a pillar for ninety-five years. There are pictures of my mother as a girl up on Fred's wagon, and there you can see him as he was, a farmer who worked on the land all his life. But most of the family photographs show Uncle Fred in a suit and tie, with a sharp-looking fedora on his head. Sunday best. Each and every Sunday, and all Sunday, was spent observing the Sabbath.

When the United Church of Canada was created in 1925, Fred was already an elder in the branch of the Presbyterian church that joined it. His father, Edward Abercrombie, farmed the land around Carman before him, and his father, Robert, came over from Ireland in the mid-1800s. There are pictures of all three men, with my mother in front, as a little girl, being supported by my Uncle Fred like a sheaf of sacred wheat.

Uncle Fred once wrote to me about the threshing bees he participated in. The wives of the men involved would congregate in the nearest kitchen and cook for the entire crew. Aunt Mae comes from a family of women who did that. Imagine the work! In a farmhouse, without air conditioning, in the middle of a prairie summer, preparing, *en masse*, the kind of food I remember Aunt Mae serving up for my family when we came to visit over twenty years ago. That day, the fare was so good, and so plentiful, that for the first time in my life I looked down to see my stomach had grown in a single sitting. It hurt! I guess it was Aunt Mae who taught me that pain and pleasure can go together.

She fell shortly after Uncle Fred passed away. So you could say she had two reasons never to get up again. Mom's cousin Ross was made executor of Uncle Fred's estate, and he's been checking in on Aunt Mae regularly since then. Now, Uncle Fred took a life-long interest in the well-being of everyone he knew, which is to say, everyone in and around Roland and Carman, plus his further-flung relations, stretching back to the beginning of this century. But Ross, who returned to the land, was especially important to him. He used to keep track of Ross's newborn calves with notes held up by fridge magnets in the kitchen. And that's what Aunt Mae was doing when Mom called.

Over the phone, Ross told Mom that the VON told him that this is the first thing Mae has shown any interest in since she fell. And so my Great Aunt Mae has taught me something else: that mourning can be an activity, and that it can get us on our feet again. You would have thought those two things couldn't go together, either, like pain and pleasure; but then, prairie people are always full of surprises.

Sweeping Gestures

It was one of my last days on the farm in France, and Paul Bournot, who had taken me on as a summer student, and I were out collecting the second cut of hay. An entire field had been swathed, and we had churned the main body of it into windrows with the *flâneur* — a kind of multiple egg beater — attached to the back of the tractor. Only the ditch grass remained, scattered at the edges, which sloped down toward the encircling fence, as if the turf were a plush cloth draped over a table of earth. It was too steep to pull the flâneur along the sides, so Paul shut off the tractor, got each of us a rake, and we began walking along the margins of the field, sweeping the sweet green stuff up to the level ground.

"No, not like that," Paul said when he saw me stop and go, stop and go, raking in staggered sections. Then he walked before me with his own rake in hand and showed me how he did it: walked and swept at the same time — a swift, integral sweep that flowed from his powerful arms to his mud-dusty peasant boots, his head tilted to one side to eye the line of scattered grass before him. Fred Astaire once said, "believe it or not, there's an artistic way to pick up a garbage can," but this was something else. Paul wasn't imposing art on an act he would normally have done awkwardly, but pulled grace out of the act itself. My jaw dropped as I watched him go, and the fields, caught up, swirled around him in praise.

That fall, when I got home to Canada, I went to the Museum of Human Movement in Hamilton, Ontario, and checked their copy of the *Encyclopedia of Rural Gestures*, or *Encyclopédie des gestes ruraux*, to see if I could find an illustration of what Paul was doing. The encyclopedia was published in the late 1700s by Jean du Cerf, a pupil of Diderot, the famous compiler of eighteenth-century France. du Cerf reacted against his master's tireless cataloguing of physical objects — books, bellows, and cannon — by issuing encyclopedias of things that did not exist as such but could, nevertheless, be seen: gestures. He believed his times to be more truly witnessed by the way a farmer handled his hayfork, or the manner in which an aristocrat raised his handkerchief to his nose, than in pictures of hayforks or handkerchiefs alone.

Like Diderot, du Cerf grew up in Langres, a walled city on a hill not more than a dozen kilometres from Genevrières, where Paul Bournot farmed. Set apart in a similar manner, the Museum of Human Movement is housed in a former cathedral on a rise of land overlooking the QEW. It contains an image bank, a showroom full of big Wardian cases on narrow wooden tables, and a library, where a rare, full set of du Cerf's encyclopedias can be found. A dancemaster curates the museum. As she took me through the showroom, I asked her why so many of the cases appeared empty.

"Here's one, for instance," I said, "that has Martha Graham's name on it, but nothing inside but air." You see, I'd never been to a movement museum before. They sprang up in Europe as court dances began to fade from memory. At the same time, Wardian cases — those big glass boxes containing worlds in small — were all the rage in the infant science of preservation. The dancemaster explained to me that the Graham case did indeed contain air — but air through which Martha Graham had passed in performance.

"Sometimes," she added, "we have to get the gesture cased right here in the cathedral." It was then that I saw the Museum of Human Movement for what it is: a temple to the ephemeral.

As I waited in the library for du Cerf's encyclopedia to be brought out, I remembered my own rural gesture that had impressed Paul the most. The summer I spent in Genevrières became very dry, and the cows had to be shunted from field to field in search of fresh grazing. Now, these were wily cows, and occasionally one of them would lead the entire herd to a pasture of her own choosing, contrary to our designs. More often, however, a headstrong cow would simply jump the single-wire, electric fences Paul had put up, into a field of unripe wheat and gorge herself until one of us went in and chased her out.

That's what I did one morning, step-hefting my ungainly rubber boots and waving a big stick, shouting "Allez, allez!" like Paul did. The errant cow bolted and took the fence like a thoroughbred, back onto the road, where she tried to blend in with the other cows. Flushed with success, I kept after her, bounding through the green wheat like an asylum escapee, when I hit the trip wire of the fence the cow had cleared and went flying — boots, stick and all — over the dry ditch and onto the road. Paul, who'd been watching, exploded into laughter. He'd sent me on this mission in the first place: my first cow chase.

He called my fall "The Plunge," and for the rest of the summer he never let me forget it. "Est-ce que tu te souviens quand tu as plongé?" he would ask, with a silver hilarity in his wizened eyes. It was the same knowing look he would give me when showing me the vaunted "Rock that Turns" — a stone attached to a string and hanging from a tree — or when, with the John Deere baler out, he'd turn to me and say, "Rien ne court comme un cerf." He may well have been the first of the postmodern farmers, a man whose self-reflection on his own rigourous circumstances unmade their boundaries continually.

I shifted uncomfortably in the chill of the museum library, waiting for du Cerf's hefty tome. All those empty, audacious cases made me want to fill their vacancies with life. I wanted to work with Paul again, see the band of burnt sienna between his collar and hair as I rode behind him on the tractor, retrace his labour with my astonished eyes. Not long after the *Encyclopedia of Rural Gestures* thudded onto the heavy furniture of the reading room, I found what I was looking for: an emblem of a farmer with his rake, like a sower in reverse, taking the fields up in his stride. Its motto ran "He swept the margin of the field." The image of Paul in my mind ran the same way, out of the museum and into the autumn sun, trailing a long line of field dancers behind him.

Arbor Vitae

A mouse fell out of the ceiling in a donut shop the other day. I had just come in for a coffee and there it was, stunned on the floor. "It came from the light fixture," a patron said. "I'll put it outside." And she did. It was cold out there, and, as I waited for my warm drink, I could see the mouse's pebbly form inching along a concrete wall just beyond the glass doors of the shop. I thought, that little thing may not survive the winter, but it isn't going to die here, in an ocean of parking lot. So I took an old container from the trunk of the car, scooped the mouse into it, and put both on the floor in the back seat. Then I drove off to Rock Chapel, to release the mouse among trees.

Rock Chapel is a park. It's part of the Royal Botanical Gardens, a collection of greenhouses, formal plots, and hiking trails which extends over twenty-five-hundred acres in Burlington, Dundas, and Hamilton, at the head of Lake Ontario. Rock Chapel drapes itself over the edge of the Niagara Escarpment, and is named after a Methodist congregation that was established there in 1822. Not long after that time, the young Egerton Ryerson, his saddle-bag bible in hand, ministered at the chapel as a circuit rider. I'm not sure what I was thinking, driving the mouse to that rocky ground. As I said, it was stunned from its fall, maybe poisoned in the first place, and winter was coming on. It wasn't like I thought taking it to a park would save it.

Two weeks earlier, I was walking through Rock Chapel when I locked eyes at about one hundred paces with those of a small dog — a black Scottie — that was waddling alongside a woman who slowed her steps to keep with her pet. You know how expressive a dog's eyes can be, but these caught mine like two eclipsed moons. So I said to the woman, by way of conversation, "That's a lot of hair on that dog!" Lame, yes, but the wee thing resembled a miniature musk ox, with its shaggy coat ballooning out from either side.

"That's not hair," the woman said. "It's water retention. See?" And she put her hands beneath the Scottie's flanks and lifted a bit. "He has lymphoma."

I didn't know what lymphoma was. "Will he get better?" I asked.

"No," she replied. "He's dying. He should have died in May — that's what the vet told us. I think he only has a few days left, so I'm taking him to all his favourite places."

I looked around. From the cedar lined ledge of Rock Chapel, you can see the watery-green expanse of Cootes' Paradise marsh, the jewel in the crown of the Royal Botanical Gardens' walking trails. The white cedars bind the eroding stone with their roots as they arc into space like coat-hooks, hung with scaly boughs. A nearby plaque tells you that some of them, although only inches in diameter, are hundreds of years old. This reminded me of the white cedars that saved Jacques Cartier's ice-bound band of sailors from death by scurvy. In the winter of

1535 they were withering away in Stadacona when Native Canadians taught them how to make tea from the cedar's leaves and bark, rich in vitamin C. Cured, the New French called the cedar *arbor vitae*, the tree of life, after the mythic one in the Garden of Eden.

As I pulled out of the parking lot at Rock Chapel that autumn afternoon, I saw, in my rearview mirror, the woman carrying her Scottie, too full of water to walk further, across the fields. She had told me she'd adopted the dog from a bad home when he was a pup. His life seemed particularly unfair to her, with its rough beginning and abrupt end. These things were in my mind as, two weeks later, I jettisoned the little mouse from its container among a stand of sumac. Rather than scurrying into the underbrush, as I'd hoped it would, it clung to the warmth emanating from the instep of my shoe. I stood up to go. I can't care for you, I said. You fell from the light, and this is the best I can do.

The Niagara Escarpment is another abrupt end: the shoreline to an ocean of air. The day I met the woman and her dog, I was walking along its ancient margin when a sound like a paperknife opening an envelope slit alongside me. I looked down to see a garter snake trailing into the leaves beside the path. It slid over and under those fallen, leafy waves — a little Loch Ness Monster — then stopped when I stopped. I hunkered down beside it. It tasted the air with its tongue.

Neither Eve nor Adam ate from the tree of life; they tasted from the tree of knowledge of good and evil. Egerton Ryerson went on to become the great educator of Upper Canada — would he not find something to praise in that taste? The snake in the Book of Genesis gets bad press, anyway: it wanted us to be wise, not eternal. The actual one beside me hugged the packed earth near the escarpment's edge, catching the last warm rays of the late autumn sun. Unlike the dog and mouse, the snake will survive the winter, and so remind me, as it winds from Eden to Rock Chapel, of the grace remaining in the gardens that last after the first one has been lost.

Prairie Wind

I stepped into the corner of the hangar and there they were: a line of cows, facing off to my left, their brown and white backs a receding range over which I could barely see. The must of urine, dung, and sweet hay filled the air, which hummed with the sound of milking machines, each suction cup spider feasting on an udder. Even though they were chained around their necks to their stalls, and preoccupied with breakfast, the cows' heavy heads lifted and turned, in a cascading rattle punched through with moos, to behold the stranger. Both the line I looked down, and the further one facing them, rippled with rolling eyes and tossing horns. For these were not polled Herefords or quaint Holsteins — they were mountain cows, and I was being inspected at the foothills of their world.

It was my first day on the farm in France — the dairy farm run by Paul Bournot. I was eager to impress my host family, but I could not hide my fear. Someone must have suggested weeding as a good way for me — pale Parisian that I was — to start. So Didier, Paul's teenaged son, gathered up hoes and a sickle and, with me perched on the fender seat, tractored out over the rolling Haute Marne hills to one of the Bournot's nearby meadows.

My fear was well founded. Imagine that a cow has given birth in a field overnight. The next morning, a woman wearing an apron opens the gate and goes to check on both mother and baby. We are on the prairies, in the 1940s, near Roland, Manitoba. The woman is sturdy and capable — she has three full-grown sons, all in the air force, whom she has brought to her second marriage. Her husband is my Great Uncle Fred Abercrombie, and her name is Ina Mae. The strong, prairie wind kicks and flutters her apron while she makes her way to the cow and its calf. As the farmers will say to each other, gathering around the gravesite afterwards, such an event happens only once in a generation, that something threatens and enrages a mother cow — she becomes "maniac" as Paul would say — and she charges to defend her newly born. I do not know if Ina Mae was gored, trampled, or simply had the life slammed out of her, but she is killed that day. It is a story my mother told me in my childhood, and it comes back with peculiar force, this first day on the farm in France.

The meadow Didier picked for us to weed was full of *chardons* — big thistles that shoot up several feet in a matter of days. We each took a hoe and started hacking away, when the half-dozen adolescent cows — too big to be kept indoors, too young for milking — that grazed in this field came over the hill to visit. Their favourite game was "I am a big bull and will prance and snort up behind you waving my horns." Whenever this happened, Didier would turn and, with a wide smile and some playful banter, raise his hoe in the air. The cow would cower. This was a boy who had gambolled among their mothers' mothers' legs as a child. He played with them as if they were

77

dogs. He could run amongst them and herd them as if he were a dog himself. Watching him, I forgot about the blisters I was tearing open in my citified palms, raised my hoe at the prancing bull wannabes, and smiled. When we got back to the house that afternoon, a gracious Didier said of me, "Il a bien travaillé."

"Il était bien terrifié," would have been closer to the mark.

Six years later, in 1991, I went to visit my Manitoban relatives. Great Uncle Fred, now ninety years old, drove into Winnipeg from Roland to pick me up. My Aunt Bea, with whom I had been staying in the city, asked when she should come to fetch me back. Fred, tall as a house and still strong as a horse, raised his patriarchal arm and grinned. This meant: Don't worry. I got into his boat-sized car with Aunt Mae, his second wife, and we drove out to the endless country.

That evening, I sat with him and Mae, and Uncle Elgin and Aunt Jean, in the Abercrombie living room after dusk, and recounted all I could of the farm in France. Everything — my cow encounters, learning to drive a tractor, the words for bales and boots and hay — set their prairie eyes afire. The pitchforks we had used must have seemed like tridents flung over a sea of time. One hot afternoon, after a slight breeze had cooled us, Didier had said, "C'est le petit vent qui fait du bien" — the little wind that does good. But I heard instead, "C'est le petit *veau* qui fait du bien" — the little calf that does good, and looked around for it. At stories like this, my great aunts and uncles laughed out of their entire landed lives.

Did I tell them the story of how Paul Bournot fetched the new-born calf, delivered overnight in a field? How he insouciantly slung it over his shoulders and, like the Good Shepherd, walked calmly back to the hangar, the mother cow lowing behind him? I must have. I had followed that little troupe, agog. After Jean and Elgin went home, I lay in Fred and Mae's upstairs bedroom, listening to the telephone wires singing in the dark.

The following morning, Uncle Fred drove me around to meet his neighbours, and then to visit the Dufferin County Museum, which is full of the effects of the farming families among whom he had lived. He recognized the silver and plate now displayed in glass cases because he had used them, ranged on well set tables at which he had been a guest. Lastly, we went to the graveyard in Carman, where Fred had grown up. We got out of the car and made our way to the headstone incised with the names Ina Mae and Frederick Snelgrove Abercrombie. The latter had no death date. Dirt had blown and caked around the former.

"There's Ina Mae," Fred said, and then bowed his large frame to tear a tuft of grass from the ground. Quick and deliberate, he brushed the encrusted earth from his wife's name. I stood behind him, the wind whipping tears into my eyes. You can never tell if you're crying or not, when it blows like that.

COUPLINGS

*My father and Frances on Home Street in Winnipeg in the early
1930s.*

Dearest Kid

There was no place to sit alone in the coffee shop, so I went up to a young woman who was writing a postcard and asked if it was all right to share her table. She said yes and so we both wrote for half an hour. When she got up to go I said, "It's nice in this day and age to see someone actually *write* a letter"; and she said, in a knowing drawl, "Yes, I'm not *wired*." Then she asked, "Why do you wear that?" and pointed to the poppy on my lapel. And I understood by the way she said "you" she meant "you Canadians."

So I told her about the poem "In Flanders Fields," and how we wear the poppy to remember those who served in the Great War and all the wars since. She then told me about a painting she used to see at a gallery in the States where she's from. "It's a field of poppies," she said, "but when you get up close, each flower becomes the face of a soldier."

A few days later, my friends Nella and Jed invited me over for dinner. It was the Remembrance Day weekend, and Jed mentioned that his grandfather, Oswald, had been in the First World War and that he still had a cardboard box full of his stuff. The next thing I knew he, Nella, and I were sitting around the open box at the table, witnessing the parade of objects that we pulled from it.

There was Oswald's identity disk, reading "No 58167 / Gascoyne / 20th Battalion Infantry / Canadian"; his three service medals; an all-metal German bayonet; his *Hate Belt*. The Hate Belt was a souvenir piece of webbing to which soldiers usually attached captured enemy badges; Oswald's is studded with the brass insignia of Canadian units — Royal Garters coiled around maple leaves, flaming grenades, roses, crowns, and guns. Jed showed me the waterproof Crown and Anchor game with wooden dice Oswald carried in the trenches and then played with Jed when he was a boy. And then there were austere 20th Battalion reunion programmes, for the dinners held annually on Vimy Night in the decades after the war.

But mainly, the box is full of postcards, dozens and dozens of them. A postcard of Oswald himself, a baby-faced farm boy cinched into khaki. Many of the cards are from a young woman named Helen, whose picture Oswald carried and whose messages, in a solid backhand, read like this:

"Three weeks till I shall be able to hear from you — cuss it all — and knowing you — little one dearest — *3* weeks probably means *5* or *6*!"

Helen became a nurse and went overseas to serve on a hospital barge. Of her crossing she writes, "Have just arrived at Falmouth — are you glad or sorry? P.S. *Very* dull crossing — no mines — no subs — no nuffink!!!"

From Rouen she writes, "I was so sick at not seeing you on the way down — still I did all I could — and chanced it. I do wonder where you are — I'm sure not very far away. I love this place; a *fine* job — Will write soon! Heaps of love dearest kid."

Most of Helen's postcards depict children, and several show Flemish boys and girls with wooden shoes and plenty of tulips. The verse on one such card reads:

> Ach, noddings,
> noddings can I do,
> but vish, und vish,
> und vish for you!

On the back, Helen added, "If wishes were fishes — I'd swim to you — darlingest little one; Good bye kid."

As Jed, Nella, and I read Oswald's postcards out loud to each other it became clear that he was a lousy correspondent. His mother, his sister, his buddies, and of course Helen, all complain about not hearing from him. On September 4th, 1916, his mother wrote:

"Just got your long looked for letter to-day & it is 5 weeks since we had a letter but 2 weeks ago we had a telegram from Ottawa to say you had concussion of the face from the Bursting of a shell & you may know how anxious we were waiting for more news & I am so glad it is no worse than a broken nose but that is bad enough & if it doesn't look any worse than Dad's it won't look so bad for you know Dad had his nose broke some years ago." The margins of this letter are fretted with X's for kisses, as if Mrs. Gascoyne had to fence her words off from the world her boy was in.

Indeed, the boys of 1916 were kept away from words. Enlisted men were not allowed to keep diaries, and their letters were censored by the officers commanding them. In the spirit of suppression, the army created the Field Service Post Card, a generic form that gave soldiers the following options:

> I am quite well
> I have been admitted into hospital: sick / wounded

I have received your: letter / telegram / parcel
Letter follows at first opportunity
I have received no letter from you: lately / for a long
    time

The men crossed off the lines that did not apply; if they added anything original, the card was destroyed.

Oswald had over a dozen of these cards, unaddressed, unmarked, that he carried with him at the front, meaning to send them to his mother, his chums, his girl.

So what did Helen do, spirited Helen on her hospital barge, somewhere along the Seine? Not hearing from Oswald, she designed her own "Canal Service Post Card." At the table, I read her invented options aloud to Jed and Nella, including the ones she'd crossed out:

I am quite well
I am anything but well
I am fed up
The barge is still afloat
The barge will not be afloat long
We have had a new patient
We shall never have a new patient
The canal smells
The canal does not smell
The weather has been wet
The weather has been cold
The weather has been windy
The weather has been all the last three, "and then
    some"
I hope to come home soon
I don't hope to come home soon
I never hope

Jed can't tell me what became of Helen. She and Oswald did not marry. And, like most veterans, Oswald never spoke of his wartime experiences to his children or his grandchildren. Still, we found another postcard showing a soldier and his sweetheart on leave, and on the back Oswald had written, "Helen and I are in London having a fine time / Feb. 17 1917." That card, too, was unaddressed.

It was late and the three of us had to go to work the next morning, so Nella carefully re-sealed Oswald's effects in Ziploc bags, and we placed everything back in the box. We all looked at each other. It had been quite the Remembrance Day. I wanted to go back to the young woman I'd met in the coffee shop and tell her she was right. If you get close enough, the poppies do have faces.

Abandoned Love

I went up to Rotblott's the other day, looking for some chicken wire. Rotblott's is a hardware emporium, sandwiched between a Harley-Davidson dealership and a new condo, on Front near Bathurst Street. That end of Toronto is an industrial neighbourhood gone to seed. A driving range has been planted in the CN marshalling yards, its giant fence echoing the huge gasworks enclosures that used to brood over the railway corridor. Rotblott's is in a low, one-storey brick shed, painted bright yellow, with a sign that proclaims: DISCOUNT WAREHOUSE since 1917.

They only had chicken wire by the roll; all I needed was a four-by-two-foot sheet. So the salesclerk said, "Why don't you try the scrapyard next door? Just go to the office and ask for Mike Greenspoon."

I went outside and turned up the alley I hadn't even noticed before that runs between Rotblott's and the scrapyard office. I pushed the door partly open and knocked. "Mike?" I called. A man came from somewhere inside, dressed like a winter thaw, full of greens and browns, wearing rubber boots; he looked as if he'd seen his share of life's debris, but had come out the kindlier for it.

I told him what I wanted. He said, "There was a piece of that stuff I kept for the longest time, and I think I just threw it away — but maybe not." We went out together.

There's a ground scale the size of a small truck that fills the entire laneway; stepping on it, the earth moves beneath your feet; on the other side, you're in a different world. "What do you need the wire for?" Mike asked, as we picked our way across the slush and mud of the yard, toward archipelagos of oil drums, set against a coastline of cast iron, sheet metal, and — for all I knew — shell casings from the First World War.

"I'm cat-sitting for a friend," I replied, "and I have a pet turtle that lives in an open aquarium. I need the chicken wire to cover the top of the tank to protect it."

I couldn't make out what Mike thought of this request. "How long have you had your turtle?" he asked.

"Ten years."

"How big is he?"

"The size of my hand," I said, and then, as I always do in response to that question, stuck out my hand with fingers splayed, imitating a four-footed creature with a long neck.

I adopted my turtle in the dead of winter from a co-worker's daughter who had abandoned it when she left for university. The night I drove by to pick it up, I rushed it outside in a large wine glass to the warmth of the car. It was the size of a loonie. When I got it home and set it up in its aquarium, I discovered it was so hollow from lack of proper food that it bobbed in the water like a bath toy. Its shell was soft as leather — and it is not a soft-shelled turtle: it is a red-eared slider — the commonest pet shop turtles there are — and it was sick.

Light, clean water, and a better diet filled my friend out a bit. I wasn't sure if it was a boy or girl, so I called it Beth — figuring I could lengthen the name to Bethune if she grew the long front claws male sliders have when they mature. But she still wasn't well, her shell a sodden cracker as she swam. So one spring day I put Beth in a basin with some water and drove her to the small animal clinic at the University of Guelph.

"Hi there, little guy!" the lab-coated vet said, who weighed her, felt her shell, and tried to get her to open her mouth with a Q-Tip. The prescription was simple: an ultraviolet plant light on a timer for basking and better food in the form of a ten-kilogram feed bag of trout chow from the local farmers' co-op. With Beth, her new hospital card, and my feed bag, I got in the car and headed for home.

I was in no hurry, so I avoided the highway and took as many winding, up-and-down sideroads as possible. About halfway back, I looked over at Beth in her basin. The water sloshed this way and that, knocking her limp, extended head from side to side like a piece of driftwood.

Gravel flew from the wheels as I pulled off the rural road and stopped the car. She couldn't die *now*! I cradled the basin out into the sun, and peered at my little green disk as if it were all the earth I would ever know.

Beth blinked. She raised her wobbly head.

"Oh you tiny cipher," I cried. "You're car sick!" I took the level highway the rest of the trip.

I thought about that journey as I carried the light fencing Mike had found for me home over the Bathurst Street Bridge. Something about my request had prompted him to ask, "Do you live in Arcadia?" When I said yes, he said, "That's my favourite building." I put two and two together. Arcadia is an artists' co-op, near the western channel on Toronto Bay, a hop, skip, and a jump from Rotblott's. Arcadians — sculptors and other lunatics like myself — must come to Mike looking for all kinds of discarded shapes. "Do you have one of those studio apartments?" he asked. I said yes. "The turtle's in front of the sky-high window," I added.

Beth became a boy, by the way. Home from Guelph, with a plant light and a mess of food, his shell helmeted into hardness and his claws shot out, he ate enough to stuff all the trout in town and has been with me ever since. The Iroquois tell us the world is Turtle: an agent of creation, the swimming island of earth. I look at mine, who peers up at me, his shell an ant hill in the water, and think, "They discarded you like we throw out everything else." But people like Mike Greenspoon, standing in Rotblott's century of scrap, are still here to help us salvage what we can.

Darling Building

I met my friend and colleague Lisa for a drink at The Paddock in downtown Toronto the other evening. She arrived, in her own words, "Felliniized," wearing a new pair of Italian glasses that were hardly needed to frame her smashing good looks. I asked her about her new publishing job, and she asked me about my writing.

"It's going okay," I said, "although it's hard to find good places in which to do it. I work in coffee shops now; I used to write in the Darling Building."

Lisa gave a start. "My parents met each other there," she said.

I practically dropped my drink. I have long admired the Darling Building. It stands at the southwest corner of Spadina and Adelaide, the heart of Toronto's garment district. When the Darling Dress Company erected this nine-storey cube in 1909, it was among the city's first *daylight factories*, so-called because its open shop floors were flooded with seamless light, pouring in through massive sash windows placed between reinforced concrete piers.

Was it possible I was about to hear an inside story from one of these castles of the rag trade? "For heaven's sake, Lisa," I exclaimed, "say on!"

In the 1950s, Lisa's father, Gordon, worked with his own father in the coal-fired boiler room of the Darling Building's basement: a darkened space — lit by a single, bare bulb. At the same time, Lisa's mother, Susie, worked as a secretary for one of the building's resident dressmakers.

One sunny, fall day, Gordon spotted his intended as she made her way through the lobby. Smit by this "younger, prettier Sophia Loren," as he called her, there followed a winter of watchings and waitings, of silent glances stolen during cigarette breaks, and shy espials in the basement restaurant.

Then, come Valentine's Day, a box of cherry-filled chocolates arrived for our Sophia. Who sent them? She enquired throughout the building.

Lisa's grandfather, the stationary engineer who ran the boilers, made no secret of his son's intent. "That boy is head over heels for you," he said when Susie asked him. "Damn, he spent nearly five hours trying to decide if you preferred nougat or cherry-filled!"

Two weeks later, when Gordon showed up for work as usual, in the dungeon of the Darling Building, he found his father grinning from ear to ear. Beside him, a bouquet of spring flowers — lilies, tulips, and daffodils — yearned in the dim light of the single, naked bulb. Susie had delivered the flowers in person, with a note and her number. Gordon was in heaven.

Lisa finished the story, we both finished our drinks, and rushed out to see the building itself, a short walk away from The Paddock. I wanted to show Lisa a detail that, for me, filled in her story. When we got there, however, I found myself staring up in reverie at a pair of windows on the fifth floor.

There, a colleague of a different colour, Shelley, recently shared a studio with three other artists. They had met at the Ontario College of Art and had spent a year painting in Florence together. Back in Toronto, they set up shop in the Darling Building, its open floors long broken up into rentable spaces. Those weekends when Shelley knew she'd have the studio to herself, she made a place for me by one of the sash windows — whose generous light is every bit as good for visual artists as it was for garment workers.

Shelley would paint, her shock of fiery hair setting off her palette, and I would write. In the pauses between paragraphs, I would stare past the sashes and lose myself in the opposite building's brick piers — just so many dun trunks in a forest of light manufacturing. Shelley and I took shelter beneath that canopy. Oh, she would work on the scaffolding of her easel with an intensity bent on reconstructing the way we might see! When the winter weather allowed, we would heave up the huge windows, as if hauling canvas for some distant place. Then the white noise of Adelaide Street flowed in, and we cast off, each absorbed by our work, in that shared ark.

Come spring, Shelley and her fellow painters had a show, and hosted a party to launch it in the studio. As the evening wore on, my friend Bob Munday and I were leaning out one of the windows, and I asked him why there were concrete barriers below, blocking off the lane nearest the Darling Building from oncoming cars.

"That's because of the coal bunkers below the street," Bob said. "The boilers were coal-fired, and the bunkers now stand empty, unstable beneath the traffic. They're to be filled in, eventually, with earth."

That was what I had wanted to show Lisa after our talk in the bar: the barriers blocking off the darkened heart of this many-mansion'd box of light, with its crenelated corners and silent sweatshops — this Darling Building.

Across the street, the Fixture Exchange sold hangers, racks, easels, and mannequins — a surviving tributary of the river of fabric that once flowed beneath the sewing machines at Adelaide and Spadina. Throughout the year, its front window would display dummies dressed as seasonal allegories: a mannequin wearing nothing but autumn leaves ran from Old Man Winter in November, for example. They closed down recently, their last display a row of severed palms, waving good-bye. The remaining seams of light manufacturing shred away from the garment district, but real people still work in the Darling Building, painting and writing, joining hands.

Promised Land

A year or so after my mother died, my father flew to Winnipeg to see his old friend Tass, who was himself attending a reunion of the Class of '49, United College. One evening, a former classmate of Tass's, up from California, asked if she could join him for supper; otherwise she'd be eating alone. Tass said, fine, but would she mind if his old pal Ernie came along, too. And that's how my father and Frances came face to face after more than half a century, with Tass assuming each had no idea who the other was.

Frances and Ernie were childhood playmates and grew up three houses apart on Home Street in Winnipeg's West End. A single photograph from that time shows a little girl who's a shoe-in for Shirley Temple, standing on the sidewalk with a skinny kid who looks like he just escaped from a Bowery Boys matinee. Frances holds a yo-yo, and between her and Dad is a wicker baby carriage with a doll inside. It is the 1930s and the Great Depression is all around them.

At that time, even families with regular incomes did not have it easy. One winter afternoon, my father wanted to go skating on the flooded, frozen, empty lot at the foot of Home Street, but his skates were so dull he asked his mother for the quarter needed to get them sharpened. Mrs. McBurney doted on her youngest, but she could not spare a dime.

"Then I'll just go out and *find* the money!" Dad fumed, as he threw on his boots, shouldered his skates, and slammed the door behind him.

Home Street was so quiet you could almost hear the fresh, falling snow swaddling the old. Dad tramped about thirty paces when he saw, in the depression of a footprint, under a diaphanous dusting of flakes, a ten dollar bill. Ten dollars. A fortune. Dad picked it up and looked around. The street was deserted. He ran back home with the money. I have often thought he and Frances found each other the same way: an unexpected treasure on Home Street, buried just beneath the tissue of time.

Frances has lived in California for most of her adult life. She followed her engineer husband there in the fifties, giving up a cutting-edge psychiatric job in Toronto to do so. In time, her husband left her for reasons he himself can no longer fathom, left her with two children to raise in a strange land, which she did quite handily, making a good living for herself as a therapist. When Dad first met her, she was spending her retirement volunteering at disaster sites for the Red Cross. She was sent to rural Kentucky following the recent tornado there. Frances is not one to flinch at difficulty.

When I first met her, at my father's apartment in Burlington, I thought — thundering cats — Dad didn't tell me she sounded so much like a Yank! I just had to get Frances talking about her Canadian roots. As it turns out, her father served with the Canadian Corps in the Great War, and her uncle was killed on the slopes of Vimy Ridge.

The morning of the attack, the Canadians came up from underground caverns dug into the chalk, while their artillery barrage poured overhead like an iron Niagara. When they'd conquered the ridge, they looked out over the Douai plain east of the German lines and saw the peace of rural France: tilled fields, redbrick villages, trains that still ran. Canada's promised land was in a foreign country.

Last winter, as my father prepared to board a flight to meet Frances in Monterey, he was being interrogated by a U.S. Customs official with ice water in her veins — or so it seemed to him. Cleared, he was picking up his bags to go when the official shot an extra question at him.

"Where did you meet your friend?"

"Where did I *meet* her?" Dad asked, his mind racing back to Home Street. He put down his bags. "Well, I'll *tell* you," he said, and got out the 1930s photo of him and Frances that he now carries in a translucent sleeve. First he showed and told the lady about the circumstances of the shot. Then he turned it over: there were he and Frances, in colour, in Monterey, she with a yo-yo in her hand and between them, a wicker baby carriage that a neighbour had just happened to have. Frances looks like, "Can-you-believe-this?" and Dad is beaming. While the official took this in, my father added that the man who re-introduced them, Tass, had also introduced him to my mother in the 1940s.

Dad put the photographs back in his breast pocket. The customs official actually wiped a tear — not ice water, after all. "Thank you for sharing that," she said.

There is a picture of Frances that I have yet to see. It's from her family photo album, and shows a golden-curled girl standing beside her uncle's name, graven along with thousands of others into the limestone of the massive Canadian Memorial at Vimy. It is the 26th of July, 1936, the day the monument, on the highest point of the ridge, was dedicated, its two giant fingers indicting the sky. On that day, Frances's father stood with her; on that day, many others stood to say good-bye to fathers, brothers, and husbands they would never see again.

This Christmas, I sat with my father at the Toronto airport, waiting to see him off. He has moved to Monterey now and is very happy. To pass the time, Dad told me how, as a young man, he ran to catch trains, springing up on one foot and swinging his weight to get on board. I love stories like that. We were also planning a time for me to visit. Dad wants me to see the places that make up his life now.

"We'll see the Steinbeck Museum in Salinas and the train museum in Sacramento," he said. And, I added silently, I'll see Frances, standing in the promise of a distant land.

Ward Story

Recently, I walked over to Huron Street, south of Dundas, in Toronto's Chinatown. It was a warm autumn evening; amber leaves daubed the sidewalks in sepia tones. I stopped at number 39 Huron — one-half of a two-storey, Victorian duplex clapped, now, with white siding: William James's house.

The William James I'm speaking of came to Toronto from England and began photographing the city in 1906. I was curious about him because the publishing company I work for just issued a book of his hand-tinted lantern slides. In James's time, if you wanted colour in a slide, you painted it on. The slides were then shown using early projectors, called magic lanterns. The result carries a city of colour from the cave of black and white. James's illuminations have lasted and are issued repeatedly from the city archives, where, in the midst of researching them, I found out where he had once lived.

It's not far from where I once lived, too — number 31 Huron. In the fall of 1985 I'd just come back from working on a farm in France and wanted to carry on with my education at the University of Toronto. I also needed a place to live, so I took a number from an ad posted on campus for a house with two women who were looking for a third person — female or male. I called, set up a time, and went down to lower Huron Street to check and be checked out.

Later that evening, I lay on the couch at my friend Alan's, where I was staying, and said, "I met two women at this house I want to live in."

"How were they?" Alan asked.

"Well," I replied, "one of them is fine, and the *other* one," I paused, "is *exquisite.*"

That was Eva-Marie, with her auburn hair and size five feet and size nine eyes. She was staying in the room with the bay window that poked its snubby nose into Huron Street. The house is akin to James's: a two-storey, Victorian twin with creaky floors and stairs that always told Eva-Marie when I was coming down to the kitchen. She would bolt: — back to her room, with whatever she'd been making — popcorn, most likely. In those days, she was half waif, but her eyes were big enough to swallow the city. Just previous, she'd studied at the Nova Scotia College of Art, where she took everything in — a dog running past her school window would be sketched in a panting flash. Once, when I did both our laundries together, her multicoloured leggings — orange, yellow, green — infused my uniform greys with the same vivifying tinctures William James took to his black-and-white pictures.

Now, among his many subjects, James photographed a Toronto neighbourhood called the Ward. The Ward lay not far from Huron, between Queen and College streets, University and Yonge. In the 1850s it was called Macaulaytown, and harboured Irish immigrants. By the turn of the century, it sheltered Toronto's growing Jewish community. The Timothy Eaton

Company always gave jobs to the Irish, but it also attracted large numbers of Jewish workers because, unique to early industries in Protestant Toronto, it allowed Jews to observe the Sabbath on Saturday mornings. Located at Queen and Yonge, Eaton's complex of manufactories and mail-order rooms anchored the Ward in place for many years. It became Toronto's dark, sparkling other at the heart of its Anglo being.

On Huron Street, Eva-Marie hung a large, cardboard star in her bay window. Like the Hebrew broadsheets once posted in the Ward, it carried a message few outsiders could read. It's not just that Eva-Marie's last name, translated, means "star" — her cardboard star was also five-pointed, one point shy of the Star of David. Its religious significance was kept hidden, much as Eva-Marie's mother, Lilian, had been hidden from the Nazis in wartime France, while half her family were slaughtered in the camps. After the war, Lilian came to Canada and raised her family in rural Quebec. I assumed at first that Eva-Marie, coming from there and with a name like *that*, was Catholic.

When I first moved in on Huron Street, I would sit up alone in my second-storey room, reading Walt Whitman aloud, sounding my yawp over the rooftops of the vanished Ward. As we became friends, Eva-Marie and I left poems for one another, hidden in the house, as we were, but wanting to be found. Eventually, we read Alistair MacLeod stories to each other in the kitchen, trading places when the going got rough — tales about miners and ghosts who sang to the living and the living who sang underground. But best of all, Eva-Marie taught me how to paint. Not to paint like an artist, but just to take a large sheet of paper and fill it with shapes and colour. She and I would sprawl on the floor together, for hours, and scrawl.

Is it any wonder Eva-Marie has become an art therapist? She now works for WRAP: the Women Recovering from Abuse Program, at Women's College Hospital. Her patients use the raw materials of art to project those things that cannot be spoken, and colour the black in their lives, hidden or broken. Long after she had left Huron Street, Eva-Marie went to study in England, where art therapy flourishes, but once she had her papers, she brought her paints, and her cardboard star, home.

Women's College stands at the head of Elizabeth Street, the spine of the old Ward, at the foot of which hangs the concrete curtain of city hall. In Canada, art therapists are as rare as the buffalo, as rare as Ward survivors — its remaining, isolated clumps of nineteenth-century row housing, cut off like wounded animals from the neighbouring herd. For the Ward was swathed like leaves of grass. In the years after James photographed them, the crowded homes, bottle dealerships, and cottage synagogues of this "ancient colony," as one observer called it, were crowbarred and carted off, to make space for hospitals, government buildings, and, ironically, the slab land of Nathan Phillips Square, named after Toronto's first Jewish mayor.

Who remembers the rough floorboards those concrete slabs cover over? Who remembers the loves that find us at our lowest points, and touch up the tombstone hues of our lives? Eva-Marie's star continues to rise over the lantern of Women's College Hospital, as she works her magic in the ancient Ward.

SLEEPERS

The Concourse Building

Bystanding

L ast winter, at lunchtime on a working day, I was heading up
Market Street, alongside the St. Lawrence Market in downtown Toronto. The market is a huge, iron-spanned shed built
atop a waterless wharf, raised over land that falls away to what
was once the shore. It is belted on three sides by an elevated,
iron-railed walkway, supported by concrete piers that lift it high
and dry from the street.

As I passed by the walkway, the sound of a scuffle made me
look up. Two men spilled out of the market's side doors,
exchanging insults and even blows. One of them staggered
about drunkenly; the other, wearing a stallworker's smock, used
each poor push and shabby kick of the drunken man as a warrant
to hammer him hard. I was halfway there when the stallworker
struck the drunken man with such force that he flew back — his
head hit the iron railing. His body bounced forward, collapsed
onto the walkway, and was still.

The man is dead, you say to yourself, when you see something like that. The shock of it concusses your perception, too — the minutes immediately following the blow are not clear to me. I know I went up to the walkway where the struck man lay; I know also that someone else confronted the stallworker, telling him what a Big Man he was; and finally, I remember the stallworker yelling back in his own defence, although you could see his frantic eyes disbelieve his own words.

Then the struck man, incredibly, sat upright, his head not smashed in, but only bruised at one temple. And I remember how oddly unwelcome that sight was, because I realized that now it was my place to talk to him, with his broken clothes and unknown injuries.

Not surprisingly, it took him awhile to stand and go over to one of the benches that face out along the iron-railed walkway. People flock to these at lunch in summer, but now it was bitter cold. Still, going back inside the market just then did not seem like a good idea. I kept looking at the man's temple and asking him how he felt; he said little. His name, he later told me, is Paul. He did not want a coffee; he did not want money. Each of the people who had gathered around made their excuses and went back to their office jobs. What to do? Someone had called for an ambulance and the police. I resolved to wait for them. Then Betsy arrived.

This woman, this businesswoman with a rich mane of jet-black hair and earrings that looked like they'd been lifted from an exhibit at the ROM, with her flowing winter coat and a Starbucks coffee in hand, had been driving by, talking on her cell phone, when she saw Paul fly into the railing. The sight had made her sick. She had called the police, and then went to get her coffee, thinking to continue her busy day. But what she'd seen would not leave her alone, so she drove back, got out of her car, and came to see what she could do. She spoke to Paul, and to me, and we all decided to wait together.

As I said, the St. Lawrence Market is built like a wharf: hints of travel hover around its waterfree piers. Its shape testifies to Toronto's origins as a port city, ribbed by narrow wooden wharves before industrial fill pushed the lake away, while its very name — St. Lawrence — reminds you that you're stationed on a vast watery corridor leading deep into the interior of the continent and far out to sea. The end of the elevated walkway on which the three of us huddled leads directly onto air.

Given that, perhaps it shouldn't have surprised me to learn that Paul is not Canadian, but Irish, and that he travelled widely before falling on hard times in Toronto. As he and Betsy shared tales of doing business in London, I thought about the Irish of 1847 who fled famine to seek prosperity in Canada. Paul had reversed the pattern, exchanging success in the old country for current ruin here. By now the paramedics had pulled up with competent, timely aid, but the police took much longer to arrive, and while we waited, Paul, still quite wobbly, began to ask me about myself as we stood beside the ambulance.

And so I told him about my own travels, and how I'd worked on a dairy farm in France one summer in order to learn French. Paul perked up at that and told me about the importance of knowing another language, and that he himself speaks Gaelic. The prejudices I had against him, due to his dress, his situation, and even his wounds, began to fall away. I am a Torontonian now: I know how to make friends and remain cold. But I was warmed by Paul's conversation, and grateful for Betsy's crucial company. You could tell time was money to her; she made it worth something else. The three of us talked for over an hour.

Strangely, Betsy's and my description of the man who hit Paul did not agree, as we spoke in turn with the police. With the law present, we sat safe inside the front entrance to the market, which was also Toronto's city hall in the 1840s; the first munici-

pal holding cells were directly beneath us. I could make out the
stallworker from where I sat as he peered occasionally at the
cops, but once it came time to describe the fight, significant
details eluded me, too. As an officer took down my version, I
wondered at how narrative changes events — even in what I'm
telling you now.

It was difficult getting away. Paul kept saying thank you,
which was embarrassing, not because he was still hammered, but
because I knew I hadn't done much for him. As witnesses, Betsy
and I couldn't even get our stories straight. But somehow, that
wasn't the point. We hadn't waited with Paul merely to see jus-
tice done, even in those old civic premises that were standing
when the Irish first came here in droves. She and I talked about
why we'd stayed so long, as she kindly drove me back to my
cubicle in the core. Something terrible had happened to Paul,
and not just at the instant that he hit the railing. What we
desired was, not so much to punish the provoked, pathetic stallworker, as to show Paul that someone gave a damn.

It may be a forlorn hope, that time taken to bide with others
in trouble will testify to their intrinsic value, whatever their circumstances. But Paul's talk of ancestral languages and business
dealings across the water did not seem forlorn to me, merely
passed-by, as he might have been, stricken on an iron-belted
walkway that leads into the sky.

Concourse Building

The Concourse Building is one of Toronto's art deco gems. Construction began in 1928, and the building received the plaudits of the press — from the *Star Weekly*, the *Evening Telegram*, the *Globe* — in the spring of 1929. It ascends to a mere sixteen stories on Adelaide Street just west of Bay, but because of the strong, vertical lines of its piers and pilasters, it shoots up like a sheaf of mechanized wheat, and seems to daunt the sky.

But it's not just the glazed, bright tiles that arrow each pier above the roof line, nor the nugget gold on that pier-punctured cornice, that make this building so special. You see, the colour decorations were overseen and executed by J.E.H. MacDonald, father of the Group of Seven, the first to dream Canada in bold, new strokes. We usually think of those guys as hanging out in Algonquin Park and sketching the elements in their rawer form. But here was MacDonald, designing the mosaic for the entrance arch, making a "concourse" of air, earth, fire, and water, through the emblems of Canadian Industry: a steam shovel, an airplane, a wheat sheaf, a plow. He said of the building, standing on Adelaide near Bay, and viewing it in the morning sun, that it "suggests to the fancy a brightly illuminated letter in a fine manuscript, beginning, perhaps, some greater chapter in our future development."

So what happened? Who would have thought that the Concourse Building would end up looking awkward? It's not just that the foyer has been stripped of ornament. In 1929, it featured Canadian poetry by then-luminaries such as Charles G.D. Roberts and Duncan Campbell Scott, chiselled directly into the stone. Their lines, along with the golden deer, fish, and birds that ran on a background of reddish-gray, as if the walls were carpeted with pine needles, have since been excised. But the exterior alone should still read the brave new way MacDonald saw it.

The deco gods that heralded the upshot of our modern cities were made of steel, their joints angled together, so that each limb would articulate with a cascade of metal taps, like a syncopated burst by Fred Astaire on a sheet of Bakelite. Their movement had not yet become the heavy, glass-plated thud of the International Style or its postmodern afterthoughts: the sort of thing you'll find all over Toronto's downtown core today. Faster than the "roaring twenties," we nevertheless seem curiously immobilized by our new technologies, to the point where we cruise the information age in complete stasis, locked behind a computer screen which seems the evil twin of MacDonald's illuminated manuscript of gold and glazed tile.

Perhaps the key to our missing motion can be caught by approaching the Concourse Building from the west — its undecorated side. There you see — near the top, above alternating bands of beige-brown brick — two huge, black eagles, clumsily pixilated in brick, and a brickwork sun, complete with heavy brick beams, and little brick birds flying around. I mean, this

112

building is really trying. It's as if someone were to evoke a sunrise by Maxfield Parish with a Lego set. But that's just it: the Concourse Building shows effort everywhere you look, no matter what it has to work with.

We can manipulate materials like never before, and not just materials, but forms of all kinds populate our urban landscape now: one only has to wander through an underground cafeteria, or stroll into latté bar or shuffle to your local bank tower to see more deco-echoing junk than ever dressed a movie set with Ginger and Fred. But the colours are all cool, not brave or new. Whatever else the glass colossi we erect to our money god are doing, they don't seem to be trying very hard: they just are hard. The manuscript that MacDonald saw the Concourse Building initializing might have read: In the beginning of the modern North American city, was the deco dream of motion, glazed paint, and steel. But take care you use these modern materials to celebrate the elements humanity came from, and not encase them, and yourselves inside them, like Fred Astaire in a food court, or eagles with clipped wings.

Crossing Over

The foot of Bathurst Street is a pedestrian's nightmare. Ten lanes of traffic lie between either side of Fleet Street and Lakeshore Boulevard, which run parallel to each other as they flow past the crosswalk: an avenue broaching Toronto as broad as any in Manhattan. Between Lakeshore and Fleet, a traffic island provides a narrow strip of relief, harbouring pedestrians who wait for the streetcar to swing along and swoop up the Bathurst Street Bridge.

I have seen automobiles stand confused in the midst of this vicious confluence, with its unequal feeder lanes making dangerous metal eddies and unexpected, screeching careens. I have seen children and the elderly crossed in front and behind by jamming traffic anxious for a few extra seconds to the next red light. And I have witnessed drivers hurling refuse and insults at pedestrians making their way across, to the larger island of co-ops, condos, and city housing plunked on the south side of Lakeshore and Fleet.

These roads run over Toronto's ancient gate: what once was the only entrance to the harbour. The current channel flows about three hundred metres south of the crosswalk, squeezed narrowly between the Bathurst Quay neighbourhood and the island airport. But in the nineteenth century, that channel coursed broadly over what is now Lakeshore Boulevard and Fleet Street, along with the residential land to the south, and the airport lands beyond. It was wide enough, in the city's early days as the Town of York, for the entire American fleet on Lake Ontario to sail through, in order to pummel the shore defences during the War of 1812.

By the 1830s, commerce was on the rise, but so was the sandbar extending from Gibraltar Point, at the furthest extremity of what we now call the Toronto Island. This bar threatened to block the entrance harbour to shipping, so a long dock was built into the water with a pierhead at its end, making a wharf the shape of a big letter T. By narrowing the harbour entrance, the wharf caused the water to flow through it faster, chasing out the sand that gathered to stop Toronto's infant industrial mouth. To honour Victoria's coronation in 1837, it was called the Queen's Wharf, and was widened, strengthened, and extended throughout her reign. Storehouses, grain elevators, and small lighthouses also sprang up on it.

If you walk west along Fleet toward the Fort York Armouries, you'll pass the only structure remaining from the wharf: its red range lighthouse, snared in a streetcar loop, on a point of land that widens between Lakeshore and Fleet as they go their separate ways. Around it, signal buildings have taken its place as markers to the city and the bay: the abandoned Molson Building, looking like the superstructure of a vast aircraft carrier, its flight deck buried in the surrounding grounds; the Loblaws Groceterias Company warehouse, whose squatiness allows it to duck beneath the Gardiner Expressway, but which otherwise draws up all four storeys as high as they can seem with lime-stone-capped, brick-buttressed piers. On the corner opposite, the Crosse & Blackwell Building, another handsomely decorated warehouse from the 1920s, asserts it hexagonal entry pavilion; and, toward the memorial trees of Confederation Park, the Tip Top Tailors Building practically erupts: a pharaonic pyramid, whitewashed and cubed, its neon title beaming from atop heady parapets, echoing and extending the tiny lighthouse opposite and its shut, red eye.

Speaking of echoes and extensions, the pedestrians who wait to cross those ten lanes of traffic — the ten lanes where the harbour entrance once flowed — do so almost precisely where the pierhead of the Queen's Wharf stood. And that narrow strip of raised concrete — the traffic island that shelters people waiting for the Bathurst car — echoes and extends the old wharf, in its function as a stopping place for vessels (streetcars in this case) entering the city from the southwest. So earlier passageways and salient features of the city displace, replace, and even resurrect themselves. We cross them out, but, in having to cross over them, remember with our movements what other bodies built and where they passed.

YMCA!

Caroline and Matthew were married in the Church in the Great Hall last September. The church is housed in what used to be one of Toronto's first YMCAs, built in 1889 at the corner of Queen Street West and Dovercourt. The Great Hall, fitted with a broad bough of pews pillar'd above the main space, refers to what was once the Y's gymnasium: the pews rest on its running track. That's where we gathered to see Caroline, in her flashing rust-red dress, and Matthew, in his matching waistcoat, exchange vows and dance the night away. I think Caroline's hair cued the colour of what she and Matthew wore; it also went well with the red brick and brownstone of the Richardsonian Romanesque building they got hitched in.

Down the street, the remaining nineteenth-century asylum wall bounding the Queen Street Mental Health Centre still keeps the old Victorian Y company. "Remember when people were either crazy or Christian?" they seem to say to each other. Torontonians generally steer clear of this part of Queen Street, just as the YMCA steers clear, these days, of prayer meetings and religious lectures. The building at Queen and Dovercourt, however, with its fairytale turret, continues to make a staid, fantastical statement in the vacuum created by our fear of the mentally troubled.

I remember running through the halls of the Queen Street Mental Health Centre late one evening. I was with someone who was a patient there, but who had also volunteered, as I had, to help out at a bingo hall to raise funds for the Toronto Tai Chi Association, and the bingo game had run past his curfew hour. Tai chi — not unlike the YMCA in spirit — hybridizes exercise and ethics. Running through those halls to get him back to his room on time seemed to underline that, even when things aren't working out in our heads, we can still work out with our bodies, feeling the institutional air against our faces.

Matthew, who has no connection with either the Y or the former asylum, took Latin dance classes prior to the wedding and, even better, wore tails for the ceremony. This meant that when he and Caroline danced their first of many dances together, he eddied and swirled behind himself, something most men, straightjacketed in suits, don't get to do very often. As the wedding guests watched him and Caroline cut their own configuration, in that nineteenth-century gymnasium-turned-church, Matthew's nineteenth-century silhouette paid strange homage to those mutashio'd tumblers who must have shouted and sprang there one hundred years earlier, evincing a robust faith in their lithe forms.

What historian Robert Browning calls "the unwashed world of the Middle Ages" had its absolute dominion delayed, for a few centuries at least, by the continued existence of the public baths at Constantinople, the capital city of the Byzantine Empire. In the ancient world, these baths provided a social, political, and physical arena combined. There, the body politic mingled with the actual, individual bodies that made it up, necessarily disarmed and, therefore, truly urbane. Here was a marriage the Byzantines preserved long after everyone else, schismatic and discreet, had forgotten the words to the physical ceremony.

Today, Toronto's downtown Y is a charitable health club, not a shelter from the ills of society or the lure of the streets. Neither chapel, nor rooms for marginalized, single men, coughing in the corners of society, survive in it. It has a pool with walls like marine bulkheads; a conditioning room where stationary bicycles hum like light manufacturing; and a weight room that, when it's not seething with testosterone, gives placidly onto downtown Toronto on steamy winter mornings.

But there is something else present which the equipment does not account for, an atmosphere in which the Byzantines would have breathed easily. Here are bodies, of all shapes, colours, sizes, and orientations, as unstraightjacketed as our society will allow them to be, in proximity, with health and community their object. Women and men making all kinds of movements, pushing through water, jumping in the gym, pumping up in the weight room, or just talking, relaxing, disarming each other with their casual company, making the Y a mental health centre, without being called one; an urbane haven, without putting on airs; and a rare marriage of bodies in its great, humming hall.

Hauling Up Ryerson

Last summer, I was interviewed for the position of managing editor at James Lorimer & Company, a small, tenacious Canadian publisher. I met with Jim Lorimer, himself, and Diane Young, his editor-in-chief, at the company's offices at 35 Britain Street — a crooked, post-industrial lane in downtown Toronto. We sat in a whitewashed room with bars on the windows and a big, black-and-white portrait of some guy on the wall. He wears a neck stock and sports a romantic, early nineteenth-century hairdo: quite handsome ... almost visionary. Eager to pass myself off as curious, I asked Diane and Jim who was depicted behind them and then, even more eager to pass myself off as well-educated, volunteered, "No, don't tell me — Is it Lord Byron?"

Diane smiled politely. It was not Lord Byron. It's the Reverend Egerton Ryerson, painted when he went to England, a young man, in 1833. The image hanging in the Lorimer office is actually a photocopy of that portrait, a little the worse for wear and jammed into an antique frame that used to hold a painting called "The End of the Day." Some time after I was hired, I asked Jim where the picture came from. "We carried it in the streets to protest the Ryerson Press being sold in the 1970s," he said — "we" being the Association of Canadian Publishers and others attached to the cause of cultural nationalism.

Ryerson was the oldest surviving English-language press in Canada and is considered, by some, to be the "Mother House" of Canadian publishing. It had originally been called the Methodist Book Room, established when the Wesleyans sent Egerton Ryerson to New York City, armed with seven hundred dollars, to buy a printing press and type in 1829. Imagine New York then, before Walt Whitman eulogized it and skyscrapers exalted it, when some New Yorkers still raised their glasses to the King behind closed curtains. Then picture young Egerton, the portrait-romantic and future champion of public education in Ontario, wandering the dusty streets of Manhattan in search of the tools with which to forge the verbal sword of the early Methodist church.

Jim Lorimer also told me that, at the same time the Ryerson Press was sold off, the Association of Canadian Publishers was resident at 35 Britain Street. They named the building after Ryerson as a memorial when the battle to keep the press in Canadian hands was lost. Until recently, a bar of wood, screwed into the wall on the first floor, read: Egerton Ryerson Memorial Building. The same legend tops the Lorimer letterhead. Britain Street is full of architects now, a perfectly civil bunch, but, as Jim once commented while he and I sifted through company archives, there's no one much left in the building now to remember Ryerson or his press. The little stick with his name on it vanished when the first floor was renovated last fall.

I came to Lorimer from the wreck of another venerable Canadian publishing house, Copp, Clark. Between them, Ryerson and Copp were responsible for most of the textbooks

English Canadians went to school with for over a century. Like Ryerson, Copp also fell prey to foreign hire, but continued under its own name for a time. Its last incarnation was on Adelaide Street, in a building long associated with the Toronto book trade. There, I formed part of a team of editors compiling directories of Dickensian proportions, including the *Canadian Almanac*, issued annually by Copp since 1847. My office mate Peter and I would amass data while the Ramones sang "I wanna be sedated" over Peter's radio — tuned eternally, it seemed, to *The Edge*.

Foreign ownership is not an evil in itself, but I'll never forget what Copp's COO told me, after the plug was pulled from the U.K. "It's not that we weren't making money," he said. "We weren't making *enough* money." Not surprisingly, the profitable *Canadian Almanac* survives, snatched up by another multinational with a nose for databases. Copp's educational arm had already been hacked off by its overseas overlords so, with the *Almanac* gone, it ceased publishing books, taking 150 years of continuous printed culture with it. I saw the Copp archives — boxes of sober readers in many languages, school editions of Shakespeare, grammars and composition books — crated up and shipped off to McMaster University, where arcane things like Canada are studied.

My colleague Patrick went by the Adelaide Street office just after things had completely shut down. Boxes of letterhead had been thrown out the front door and were blowing down the street like tumbleweed, Patrick said. I imagined the envelopes and paper with the Copp, Clark logo — an open book on a shield — caught up in those little twister winds that clustered buildings cause, strewn thick as autumn leaves over dusky Adelaide. It was as if the spirit of the company were trying to publish all that was left of it — its name — over the streets of Toronto. Maybe some of those envelopes blew their way to Britain Street.

Soon after I came on board at Lorimer, we moved from that barred-window first floor to the skylit third. Two copies of every book Lorimer ever issued, and furniture you could build a boat out of, had to be lugged to our upstairs ark. We share the floor with more of those architects, and they told me that, at first, our building was an 1870s knitting mill. You can still see a row of trap doors that punctuate the wooden floors along the wall; through these fed belts that ran the mill machines. So, in a way, 35 Britain Street has always been a house of homespun industry, mass-producing the woven word.

After we were all settled in, Diane noticed we'd left the Ryerson portrait behind, so Jim and I went downstairs to fetch it from its jailhouse room. Jim started to laugh as we hauled the ungainly frame up the stairwell. I looked back at him down the narrow passage and saw his face — lit with more than its usual urgency. Lift me up, lift me up, the portrait seemed to say. The Ryerson Press may have lost its autonomy, but the man who founded it still shapes the Canadian book trade, and not just through the publishing courses at Ryerson University. I thought of Copp, Clark's open book in a Canadian shield as a fit emblem for him, who braved the world to publish at home. Isn't that the best kind of outside interest? Edgerton's early image leans forward from the wall, now, in the Lorimer office.

GRAND CENTRAL STATION

My Remington Noiseless, with a poem it wrote.

Movable Type

When I was twenty-one I moved to New York City to study dance and acting at the Circle in the Square Theatre School. The main thing I brought with me, aside from some clothes and a handful of books, was an antique typewriter that came in its own carrying case. You may remember typewriters. They were the things we used to write stuff down with, when our hard drives were still lodged in our heads. Anyway, the typewriter was a 1930s Remington Noiseless Portable. The handy little Remington was made of cast iron and the weight of it just about yanked my arm off hauling it around, but its big black box of a case was useful. When at first I didn't get my room at the 34th Street Y, and didn't know where I was going to sleep that night, for instance, I could sit down on my typewriter in the street, and cry.

I think that was about as portable as my life ever got. In retrospect, that move reminds me of a scene from a film that's about the same age as the Remington itself — the 1937 musical

Swing Time. In it, a penniless Fred Astaire has to get to New York City in order to win enough money at the gambling tables so that he can convince the father of the woman he initially wants to marry that he can earn a respectable living. Wearing his wedding clothes, he jumps a boxcar with a buddy, who dumps all of their luggage on the tracks while running to catch the train. Fred's real talent in the film turns out to be dancing, of course, and his real partner turns out to be Ginger Rogers, who's about as broke as he is. The two of them quickly make the switch from moving to movement, and fill their pockets by dancing the screen on fire.

Just prior to moving to New York, I'd spent the summer working at Old Fort York, a historic site in downtown Toronto. There we dressed up as British infantry from the War of 1812 and drilled in the sun all summer long. We practised early nineteenth-century military evolutions, wheeling, turning about, and inscribing, with our footsteps, little circles in the fort's parade square, kind of like a human kaleidoscope, all the pieces of which were red. I sure moved around a lot, albeit in the same place, that summer. The knapsacks we wore were black boxes bound together by two white straps. When it came time to leave Fort York for New York, I bound the black case of my Remington Noiseless in the same way, with two bands of white tape, to keep it from falling open, like Fred's luggage did.

When I wasn't in dance or acting classes, or working at a newsstand in Greenwich Village, I would chase the cockroaches off the narrow table in my little room, uncase my typewriter, and tap away into the night. I hadn't yet seen *Follow the Fleet*, another Astaire-Rogers musical in which Fred expresses the same rhythms typing up the script for a play he wants to stage that he does tap dancing across the deck of a battleship. But I had my own military dance examples to draw upon and, furthermore, was blessed with the ability both to move around a great deal in the small spaces which held our classes and also to move entirely from one big place to another. The kind of movement I wanted most, however, and got from having sought the first two kinds so avidly, was the freedom to move anywhere I wanted in my head, whomping out the syncopation to that on my Remington Noiseless Portable.

Funny, but I don't think I've ever felt better, bawling on that encased typewriter on 34th Street. Bear in mind how naive I was. I'd only just discovered that New York was where you found the Statue of Liberty (I'd thought, from watching *Planet of the Apes*, that it was on an abandoned beach somewhere). I thought Greenwich Village was a hamlet in the country. The Empire State Building, which is also on 34th Street, I knew because King Kong fell off it, but otherwise, New York was about as big and scary a place to me as anywhere is ever likely to get. I was terrified. And terribly, terribly happy.

Fightmaster

I first walked in the door of the Toronto Tai Chi Association in the spring of 1984. It was founded by the late Master Moy Lin-Shin, a Taoist monk from Hong Kong, in the early 1970s. I'd just come from taking a pack of dance, movement, and stage combat classes in New York City, as part of my training as an actor. Before I left the big city, my closest friend at the Circle in the Square Theatre School, John Siemans, cocked an eye at me during our good-bye walk through Greenwich Village and said, "Ward, you should do tai chi." John was a close friend, but on this occasion I didn't know what he was talking about.

Still, I trusted his intuition, so when I got back to Toronto I looked in the Yellow Pages under tai chi. I found nothing. Then I turned to martial arts, where I found a listing for the Toronto Tai Chi Association. I wasn't aiming to attack anybody, and tai chi is pretty gentle stuff to watch, but my beginning instructor at the Toronto club did remind me a little of B.H. Barry, who had taught us, in New York, how to tumble and fight without cracking our heads or drawing blood. "B.H.," as his students affectionately call him, is a fightmaster. Some of you may remember when the Three Musketeers films came out, with Michael York, thirty years back ... B.H. did the fights for those.

He is a remarkable instructor. Our first session with him, he had each and every terrified one of us running and tumbling head first onto the floor, with an arm extended to ensure that we dove and flipped ourselves upright again as we ran. I remember how John would complete those headlong somersaults, clawing the air like an acrobatic cat. And I remember too how B.H. used to end our sessions on Friday mornings, after we'd been beaten up, in a staged way, by most of our friends. We would gather round him meditatively, and he would recite to us the lines from the science fiction book *Dune* about overcoming fear. "I will not fear. Fear is the mind-killer. Fear is the little death that leads to total oblivion ..." he would quote, then send us out into the roar of Manhattan.

Toronto is a quieter town, and Master Moy's entrance into my life was far less dramatic. He would poke around at the Bathurst Street club while classes were going on, looking like a lost janitor, but when he stopped to correct a student, the earth could move. People who don't do tai chi have a hard time imagining how anything that slow can be so demanding, but whenever I practised, I would sweat buckets. I wasn't alone in that, so it was common, after class, for a group of us to go and eat to restore our strength. This would happen even if we finished exercising at, say, ten in the evening.

One of those late suppers changed my life. About twenty of us, Master Moy included, piled out of the old synagogue on Cecil Street where we'd been working out and went to an underground restaurant on Dundas east of Spadina. It was hot August; as we made our way through Chinatown, boxes of offal stacked in back alleys filled the night air with pungent decay. By this time, I had spent two years trying to get an undergraduate degree in English while holding down odd jobs and moving every four months. I'd about had it. That summer, I was working for the tai chi club, so I guess Master Moy had seen enough of me to figure out how unhappy I was.

"What are you going to do in the fall?" he asked through an interpreter.

I looked up from my rice and said, "I don't know. I hate school, and English is useless."

"You should study what you want," Moy said. "Go back to school this fall and I'll pay your tuition."

"I don't know what to say," I said, taken off-guard and a little spooked at the suddenness of the offer.

"Say yes," the interpreter added on his own, "before Mister Moy changes his mind."

So I accepted, and Moy Lin-Shin proved in that instant both that English *was* useless, since he didn't need it to get his message across, and that it wasn't, since I did. I went on to start my first full-time year at the University of Toronto that fall, and graduated two years later with an honours degree — in English. I hadn't really meant what I'd said about hating school, either, which Moy must have guessed. I'd just had the wind knocked out of me.

But it was classic Moy to push someone like that. You'd be plodding along, eating your rice, and bang! He'd sock you with an offer you couldn't refuse. If you've ever seen tai chi sped up into its martial arts mode, you'll know what I mean. It's amazingly fast, and scary as all get-out. Master Moy practised the same kind of movement socially. "Fear is the mind-killer," he might have said. "Go get your degree."

That imperative had its origins in New York City. "You're too smart to be an actor," one scene instructor told me. "I think you should go back to school." I agreed, eventually. Before leaving the Circle in the Square, I went up to B.H. Barry after combat class and told him I didn't want to act. He laughed out loud and hugged me. That was, as with John's and my good-bye walk, the best send-off a roving student could have had. How could I have guessed that another fightmaster, from the other side of the world, was up ahead, waiting to knock the wind into me?

Last Call

Every now and then, the desire to see New York becomes too much for me, and I have to go. Not to visit anything in particular, just to walk in Manhattan's shadow again — up and down the wide, spinal avenues, ribbed with cross streets — and feel reduced to my proper proportions by those staggering buildings that grate against the sky. I studied acting there as a young man, and was so happy I've never gotten over it. Later in life, I went to graduate school at Rutgers University, in nearby New Jersey, where I met my friend Amy. Whenever I visit now, she and I meet in Manhattan; we do most of our talking on the sidewalks of New York.

After grad school at Rutgers, I came home to work in publishing, and started, appropriately enough, as a bookseller at A Different Drummer Books in Burlington. A Different Drummer had been my boyhood bookstore; what better place to begin my adult career? Now, one day five copies of a large, hardcover book called *Up in the Old Hotel*, by a man named Joseph Mitchell, arrived, but one of them never reached the display surfaces inside the store. Sometimes you clap eyes on a book and — before you open it, decipher its front cover or even read the back cover copy — you know that book is for you.

Up in the Old Hotel is one of those. These days, it should really be called *The Lost World*. It's a collection of story-length profiles written for the *New Yorker* in the 1930s, 40s, and 50s by a ground level reporter who crafted pages of monologue and dialogue out of encounters with New York City eccentrics: street preachers, diamonds in the rough, and, in his own words, "out and out freak show freaks." Joseph Mitchell was a long distance listener — an archaeologist of air, when Manhattan was the great gotham where all races babbled.

My acting classes had been scattered all over New York and so my fellow theatre students and I used to walk constantly. I knew nothing, then, of the city's history or of Joseph Mitchell's profiles. Nevertheless, the overpowering impression I received was that Manhattan had been built by a people wholly vanished from their own accomplishments. Perhaps it was in that spirit that, this spring, Amy and I visited the new National Museum of the American Indian. Each object within it is assigned multiple interpretations by several Indigenous curators. Between a horse mask and a turtle basket, say, and the new voices interpreting them to us, lay a river of time, successfully bridged. If these vanished peoples can become present again, why not those of mighty Manhattan?

Stepping down from the museum, Amy and I decided we could use a beer. Now, Joe Mitchell's first essay in *Up in the Old Hotel* profiles the longestanding saloon in New York. At the time Mitchell wrote it in 1939, McSorley's Old Ale House (which was called "Old" even when it was new) had been in business for seventy-five years and was something of a landmark, located both on the edge of the Bowery and firmly in the nineteenth century. Inside McSorley's, almost nothing ever changed. There was sawdust on the floor; onions, crackers, and cheese for lunch; and a sign above the entrance to the back room that read BE GOOD OR BEGONE, placed by Old John McSorley himself.

Actually, when Joe Mitchell wrote his story, just about *everything* in McSorley's dated back to Old John's time, because his son, Bill, had screwed every portrait, newsclipping, and curiosity of his father's to the walls after he died. Bill had an aversion to change that must have stemmed from a heady mix of habit and grief. I had been to see the saloon one winter day during the time I studied acting and for years carried around a mental image of the interior of the bar, unchanged from its earliest days. But even that was a long time ago, and now, I figured, standing there with Amy in the spring sun on the steps of the Museum of the American Indian, not only must I have fabricated my memory of McSorley's from some old photo I saw, but it would be a minor miracle if the bar still existed at all.

Anyway, we got in a cab and went up to 15 East 7th Street, and there was McSorley's Old Ale House, just where Joseph Mitchell had left it. We walked in the door. A little sea of sawdust covered the floor; onions, crackers, and cheese were on the board for lunch; and a crude sign reading BE GOOD OR BEGONE hung over the table in the back room where Amy and I sat. The wood of the walls — what little of them you can see behind Old John's memorabilia — is stained a deep brown with a century of tobacco smoke and coal dust. The potbellied stove where the old men used to warm their ale in winter is gone, but otherwise, McSorley's looks as if it's been preserved in its own amber brew.

Joseph Mitchell tells us that "Old John believed it impossible for men to drink with tranquillity in the presence of women ... and said that 'Good Ale, raw onions, and no ladies' was the motto of his saloon." The ale remains, and the onions you get with lunch are still raw (if sliced; Old John ate them whole), but the last part of John's motto has changed — thank goodness! The only tranquillity I had on that trip was talking to Amy in McSorley's, with my onion-breath and all. We shared our stories over their house ale, putting our cigarettes out on the floor as instructed by the manager. He seemed aware of the importance of his charge, so I told him I was visiting because of the Joe Mitchell story. "I met Joseph Mitchell three times," he said. "He used to come in here." The manager looked about my age. At that point I realized that McSorley's isn't just preserved, but alive.

When I first read *Up in the Old Hotel*, I became so excited by it that I spoke several of the profiles onto tape for my father to hear. I even wrote to the author, care of his publisher, thanking him for allowing his writing to be re-issued. Shortly after that, I received a very polite form letter telling me that Joseph Mitchell was no longer able to read very well, but that he was thrilled at the reception of his book and with the number of letters he was receiving. He died shortly after, knowing his work would last. When Amy and I showed up at McSorley's at three in the afternoon, it was full. When we left at five, staggering happily into the uproar of the city, it was packed.

Haida

I was having lunch with my friend Alexandra the other day and
told her I had just spent three hours on board HMCS *Haida*.

"Is that the ship that's at Ontario Place?" she asked.

"Yes," I said, heartened that she knew it. I had figured
Alexandra — a published poet with her own rock band — had
better things to do than hang out with old destroyers.

"I love that ship," she said with a smile. "Every time I drive
by, I wave at it."

She is eye-catching — *Haida*, I mean. Her sleek and sober
form, festooned with pennants above a battleship gray hull, has
hunkered along Toronto's lake shore for as long as I can remember. The ship is a floating museum. Her curator, Lieutenant Peter
Dixon, gave me the lowdown on "Canada's largest artefact."

HMCS *Haida* is a Second World War Tribal Class destroyer.
The Tribals were hard-hitting and swift, named after strong
Aboriginal tribes, like *Huron* and *Iroquois*. "Magnificent in
appearance, majestic in movement, and menacing in disposi-

tion," is how one contemporary admiral described them. During the war, *Haida* formed one of a pack of night brawlers that sped into the English Channel before and after D-Day. Concealed by darkness, flashless gun powder, and smoke screens, she and her fellow Tribals mixed it up with enemy ships by the light of parachute flares called starshells. *Haida* was tough and lucky, captained by a man whose last name, aptly enough, was DeWolf. She sent more than her share of Nazi belligerents to the bottom.

A colleague from my time in the history business, Ed Anderson, volunteers on *Haida* as a guide. He took me around the ship from turreted bow to ensigned stern, from oily engine room to open bridge. An elevated catwalk spans *Haida* amidships, so that her crew could traverse her in a high sea without being washed overboard. Ed turned to me up there and, like the good interpreter he is, asked me to imagine the waves of the North Atlantic crashing over the ship's waist below.

I looked down. The last time I'd been on a catwalk was in the Circle in the Square Theatre on Broadway in New York City. I was studying acting there, and had been given my oddest student job ever — to watch a defective sprinkler valve during productions of *The Caine Mutiny Court Martial*. In the event of fire, I was to turn the valve by hand and douse the audience below, much as the crew of *Haida* must have been doused many times by the water breaking over her sides.

That was over fifteen years ago, and *The Caine Mutiny* was more resonant then in the minds of the audience than it would be today. It's the story of a worn-out captain, Queeg, who commands a U.S. Navy minesweeper — the *Caine* — during the Second World War. Once at sea, the officers on board decide Captain Queeg is a sick man and rise against him. During the trial at the war's end, Queeg is disgraced by a sharp defence lawyer, Barney Greenwald. Afterwards, Greenwald stumbles into a celebration the acquitted *Caine* officers are holding, drunk as a skunk.

I've never forgotten the scene that followed, night after night, as I clung aloft to the catwalk and peered down from the darkness onto that Broadway stage.

Who was standing guard on this fat, dumb, and happy country of ours, Greenwald asks the officers, when you and I were chasing after money? Stuffy, stupid Prussians like Queeg. And after we joined up and were learning how to fight, who was stopping the Nazis from melting the Jews into soap? he asks again, for his own mother had narrowly escaped the camps.

"Queeg deserved better at my hands," Greenwald finishes. "I owed him a favour, don't you see? He stopped Herman Goering from washing his fat behind with my mother."

There were no Captain Queegs on board *Haida* during her term of service, but like Queeg, she is definitely worn out — she is rusting out along her waterline. If her hull isn't repaired within five years, Peter Dixon expects she will sink. The nearest dry dock is in Port Colborne, and it would be a simple matter of towing *Haida* to it, were it not for the four-lane causeway built behind her that baulks her exit to Lake Ontario. Peter figures it will take $5 million to either demolish the causeway, or to dry-dock *Haida* where she lies, in the basin-sized bay she shares with a swarm of whining bump boats.

Peter loaned me his copy of the book on *Haida*, an old out-of-print paperback that chronicles her scrapes and escapades during the Second World War. The story that struck me the most was when she stopped to rescue survivors from her sister ship, *Athabaskan*, torpedoed in the English Channel during a night engagement. Dawn was fast approaching, and *Haida* had to speed back to Plymouth to avoid enemy aircraft.

As she got underway, two of her crew down in the scramble nets at her side were swept into the water and sucked beneath her hull. Their shipmates feared the men would be cut to pieces by the huge, spinning propellers that now stand pillar'd beside

Haida like mutant blenders. But the men were not cut to pieces, and in the morning, they were picked up by *Athabaskan*'s drifting launch. *Haida* had spared her sinking heroes.

In five years time, will we be able to say the same towards *Haida*? What will we do the morning she lies sideways in her cell, the bump boats droning around her sunken hull like flies on a beached Leviathan? Will we cut her up for scrap then, this old scrapper? Will we leave her disgraced in the dock like Queeg?

Haida deserves better at our hands. We owe her a favour, don't you see? Her sleek and sober form stood guard on this fat and happy country of ours, and she is the last of the Tribals that did so. It remains to be seen whether, like Alexandra, we will continue to wave at *Haida*, or whether her iron brow, which has been washed by the waves of every ocean on earth, will finally slip beneath them.

Gotham Lullaby

I was perched on a lip of marble in the biggest room in Canada and my life was over: I had just left acting school in New York, and sat in a windowsill beneath the coffered ceiling of Union Station, which had closed on me like a vast chest. I knew I did not want to be an actor; I did not know what I was going to do next. I couldn't move.

One of the reasons I had studied acting in the first place was that it scared me. And the part of it that scared me the most was not voice classes in uptown studios, nor scene work in the basement of the Circle in the Square Theatre on Broadway, nor even stage combat: the part that scared the bones out of my body was dance. We had had three different dance classes a week, on the sprung floors of an old tenement building in Hell's Kitchen in Manhattan. The best of these was simply called "Movement."

The teacher's name was Randolyn, and the first thing she said to us was "I am interested in your awkwardness." She sat like a folded eagle and moved as if the air were a manuscript she alone could illuminate. She told us how Fred Astaire, who was still alive at that time, pointed his way with his fingers; she told us of a rain dance she did in Louisiana under a clear blue sky, bringing on clouds and thunder; she told us we should dance in our kitchens.

She played spooky songs by Meredith Monk during warm-ups. My favourite was "Gotham Lullaby," which somehow helped us all to stretch that much further. When one of my class-mates pounded his legs with his hands because he could not reach his toes, Randolyn crossed over to him and said patiently, forcefully, "Don't, ever, do that." And then, with the tenement windows wrested open to the great city, its armfuls of dust fin-gering through the light, she would swoop down the floor and we would follow, an awkward gaggle, her waddling retinue.

Randolyn asked us to choreograph our own solos. I had to rehearse mine in my room at the 34th Street Y, which was the size of a generous coffin. Since I could barely move, I slapped a pounding tune on my Walkman and, with my feet nailed to the floor, imitated what it was like to both walk through and be Manhattan at the same time. I was skyscraper and pavement, pedestrian and rooftop. Shut up in violence, at one point I dropped so hard on my knees that the class gasped.

Randolyn watched all this pacifically. Afterwards, she said I should be a choreographer. It was my turn to gasp. She also said I might like to buy some knee pads.

Then one day, towards the end of term, she taught us how to waltz. I must have volunteered to be "the example," because all I can remember from that class is locking onto Randolyn's eyes as the room spun around us. And although I cannot waltz to save my life, she taught me at that moment the best lesson. As we whirled in Hell's Kitchen and the room went wild with faces, windows, walls, and mirrors, she held me upright with one hand on my spine while the other rested in my left, and I was, strangely, still in her moving sphere, her face grave as a sermon, her eyes clear as a Sunday bell.

The day I left Manhattan I sat on my typewriter in Grand Central Station, my head in my hands. I heard a click and looked up. It was a photographer, who had just turned me into a poster child for despair. Arrived at Union Station in Toronto, I watched the human figures passing between the panes of glass that window either end of the concourse. All movement seemed walled off from me. In order to get myself off the ledge, and onto the next stage of my life, Randolyn, in a waking apparition, pointed her way across the huge room and, spreading her wings, feathered me down to the hard floor. I walked. I could still walk.

Seventeen years have passed since that time. I found the best way I could preserve my fledgling dance heritage was to learn the tai chi set, a moving meditation that is particularly good for your knees. This summer past I was doing the set on the roof of the downtown Toronto YMCA, when a girl came out, and, instead of running around the track up there like most people do, began running through an elaborate dance routine.

She crouched, she flung, she bundled herself into fists and sprang into half pirouettes. I was able to catch all this because she decided to work only a few feet away from me. I kept going through my motions and said nothing. All you could hear was the soft clop and stomp of her small shoes as she started, stopped, stepped, and spun. When she was really stuck and had to recollect her routine, she walked in a full circle around me.

You don't get to witness something like that everyday. When I was finished the set, I gathered up my courage and asked her:

"Is that your choreography?"

"Ye-ah!" she gushed.

"It's good."

"Thanks!" she replied, as if I'd just given her an "A."

As I descended the Y's clerestoried stairway, I realized — her dance was great, but — I was interested in her awkwardness.

STEAM

Dad and his iron twin, St. Thomas, Ontario, 1998.

Pistons & Plastrons

Last spring, my father and I took a ride on the South Simcoe Railway, which runs on a branch line between Tottenham and Beeton, Ontario, southwest of Lake Simcoe. It's a history train. We rode in day coaches from the 1920s, pulled by a CPR steam engine, Number 136, that was built in 1883. Millions of Canadians have, in fact, seen this engine, because it chugged its way across the televised version of Pierre Berton's *The National Dream*, a stand-in for all the steam locomotives that were. The South Simcoe Railway Heritage Corporation has done a fine job of preserving and keeping it in running condition.

My father worked for the CPR in the 1940s, 50s, and early 60s. He remembers the age of steam; he saw it give way to the diesels. Dad doesn't mind the new engines, but they lack the living mimicry the steam ones had, panting like winded animals, herded into the stations he knew in Winnipeg, Dryden, and Portage La Prairie. But it isn't just sound that sets steam engines apart from their successors. Think of the machines we come into contact with now, cars and computers: where are their moving parts? Under the hood or just plain gone. But a steam engine, like a good performer, externalizes everything it does: pistons punch out around whopping huge wheels weighted for momentum, while the train trails a Samson-like stream of steam hair.

The conductor of the Simcoe train, with his round spectacles, gray beard, and waistcoat, looked like your average, dour, nineteenth-century railway employee, but in narrating the trip for us, he was as droll as they roll. The train goes backwards for the first half of its run, because there's no wye for it to turn, but according to him, the real reason we travelled so slowly between Tottenham and Beeton was that if we derailed from excess speed we'd be "off the beaten track." This is the kind of humour my Dad actually finds funny. The conductor also told us another slow thing about Engine Number 136: It has a curious and bizarre mascot, a turtle, which, he claimed, watches the train go by from atop a rock in Beeton Creek, which runs alongside the tracks.

I like turtles. I have one at home. I know they watch things. Heck, they're turtles: what else is there to do? But I was a little suspicious about the existence of this mascot. Lethargic, squamous, with brains the size of shriveled raisins, turtles nevertheless know their vibrations, which always mean: trouble! They'll dive for cover at the snap of a twig twenty yards distant. What could cause more shudders in a cold-blooded terrapin's heart than a century-old steam train, thundering along its iron road?

Imagine my surprise, then, upon seeing a turtle hunkered on a rock in the middle of that tiny creek. I stood up and saw it as we shunted backwards, a large snapper, almost as broad as the brook itself. It stared vacantly at the Simcoe train, in the way snappers do, practically drooling out of its razor-edged mouth. They strike this permanent pose when underwater, to lull and lure you, if you're a fish, into going inside their mouths for a

148

piece of that wiggling-thing-is-it-a-tongue?! But this one, perched in the open air, lured me another way, back in time.

You see, snappers are the oldest turtle species left on earth, but in 1953, my father, at age twenty-eight, was made the youngest Express Agent in the CPR. Express Agents are especially unlike turtles in that they're responsible for freight that has to move fast. As the Simcoe train crawled backwards, Dad told me about the things they used to do to avoid stopping major trains in the station, if all they had to do, say, was give a message to the engineer. Dad would hold out this hoop on the end of a long pole, with the note for the train attached, and the engineer would lean out from the oncoming engine, spearing the hoop with his arm and taking it up, pole and all. Once he'd snatched the message, the engineer would cast the pole back to the ground up ahead, where someone would retrieve it for next time. It wasn't part of an Express Agent's job to do that; Dad just found it fun.

The day-coaches the Simcoe train pulls are the kind that took him up to Winnipeg Beach for weekends by the water, when he was a boy. So it was easy to see, even as we reached Beeton and started back, going forwards this time, that Dad was travelling in several directions at once, remembering times when both the entire country and his young life lay before him like two shining rails running alongside each other. Somewhere along that line he and my mother found the time to raise me and my brother, while his hair turned white as the steam of the Simcoe train. As we rattled alongside Beeton creek, Dad asked if the turtle was still there, my own ancient shape, my own armoured twin. It was. It hadn't moved an inch. But Dad has speared me up, and carried me on board his life, without having to stop.

Bar Hopping

I was walking along Queen Street West with my friend Claudia the other evening. Just before reaching Bathurst Street, she nipped into a convenience store, and I waited for her outside. Close to me was a small knot of elderly men who looked as if they'd seen their share of Toronto street life. What caught my ear was one of them kept saying "you oughta' tell that to Mike Filey." Mike Filey, of course, is a well-known local historian. I wondered if he knew these men or if his name served as a kind of reliquary to them, a place where old stories should go. Then Claudia came back out of the store; she hadn't found what she was looking for. It was my turn to ask her if she could wait a minute. She did, for a moment, then said she'd be back and went off to a nearby drug store.

I leaned into the air surrounding these old guys to try and figure out what oughta' be told to Mike Filey, but all I could catch was something about a waiter and a waitress who had met untimely ends in 1947. Still, it was clear these men were creating an odd pocket in time, a hollow rock in the stream of squeegee kids, goth youth, and ravers that swirls around the crossroads of Queen and Bathurst. I can never forget that there was once a military blockhouse standing on what is now the southeast corner, in a clearing hacked out of the bush, guarding the northwestern approach to the town of York almost two hundred years ago. Kitty-corner from that site now, St. Christopher House, a community centre, maintains another kind of outpost: their Meeting Place for street people, complete with showers and laundry facilities. And just down Bathurst Street is the old Paddock, which boasts the longest bar in the city.

At least, that's what Tim Henshaw told me. Tim is the chef at the newly reopened Paddock. I was sitting with him after hours at the formica tables that now fill the non-bar portion of the restaurant like flat-headed pawns, and he said The Paddock first opened in the 1940s. In my time, I simply knew of it as the vilest-looking dive in town. After it closed in the late eighties, you would have thought that anyone wanting to reopen it would simply flush any associations with the past down the newly scrubbed toilets. Instead, they kept the signature tile with the jockey cap on the recessed entry outside, and inside, peeled away four decades of neglect to reveal a superfine deco beverage room with an L-shaped bar waiting to cradle you in the crook of its dark arm.

Tim is a first-rate chef, and The Paddock is worth anyone's patronage. I came by for dinner a week or so later with my pal Mychol to savour the fare. Mychol is the IT coordinator for St. Christopher House, that urban angel a stone's throw away. After ordering, we fell to admiring the décor, and I got curious about the surface of that bar. Tim had told me it was special. I went up to its shiny black top and rapped on it. It was better than special — it's Bakelite: the dream plastic of the jazz age. You can still catch bits and pieces of old Bakelite in the city: the shelf to an empty phone booth, desktop accoutrements in yard sales, but here was a whole barful of the stuff, dark and polished and ready to dance on.

Dancing and Bakelite go together like Fred Astaire and Ginger Rogers, because they did a lot of their dances on surfaces made out of it. By the 1940s their partnership was over, but Fred was still hoofing, and in 1943 he starred in a remarkable film called *The Sky's the Limit*. Remarkable for him, because it contains the most exhuberantly destructive dance he ever did. He plays a fighter pilot who must return to the front without telling the woman he loves that he's a war hero rather than a bum. You see, he doesn't want her to love him for what he does. This makes precious little sense, but somehow goes with Astaire who, for all his fame, had a decorous horror of self-promotion and was embarassed by his own immaculate performances.

Anyway, Fred finds himself in a tropically decorated bar the night before he's to fly back to the Pacific theatre. After tossing off "One for My Baby" — which was, like so many classic songs, written for him — he staggers around between tap spatters and then, inspired, hops up onto the surface of the bar at which he's been drinking. There, he skids from one end to the other like a condemned man on a coffin lid. The sound of his horseshoed heels was never more like machine-gun fire than it is now. Things get ugly as Astaire smashes every stacked glass in sight; actually, things get superlatively smashing: he destroys as a dancer, not as a drunk. He finishes by hurling a stool into the mirror behind the bar, and then slumps at the counter, spent amidst the ruin of war.

Back at Queen and Bathurst, the old men made their way into one of the Queen Street coffee shops that echo the lunch counters which used to honeycomb the city — you know, the kind that would have Maple Leaf Cafe on the window but be known as "Charley's" to the locals. Claudia came out of the drug store ... she'd found what she was looking for: one of those chocolate eggs with a toy inside. It was for me. Claudia's the kind of person who will not only wait for you for seemingly no good reason, but will use the time to get you a present. I caught ahold of the long braid that cascades down her back — figuratively, of course — and we flew to our own coffee shelter along Queen. Behind us, the hooftaps of night cops on horseback rounded the corner towards The Paddock. There may be longer countertops in the city, but I'd say that Bakelite bar stretches pretty far back, just the same.

House of Industry

The first time I saw the Hamilton Steam Museum was almost ten years ago. I was just about to attend graduate school south of the border. Serious work, it seemed to me then, was something you did far away. Still, I wanted to mark my last days in Canada as significant. I don't remember how I heard about the museum — an old Victorian waterworks in the middle of nowhere — but I cajoled my dad into visiting it with me.

So we arrived at the Romanesque pumphouse holding two massive beam engines that used to draw water from the lake, and I was surprised to see a familiar face: Dallas Wood had done research at Historic Fort York years ago, when I had worked there. Now he was curatorial assistant at the steam museum. I don't remember much about the tour he gave that day save that he was thorough, explaining to us that the same stationary engineer, James McFarlane, had run the works for its entire effective life, from 1859 to 1910. That and the fact that the beam engines didn't work — you had to inch their twenty-two-ton fly-wheels forward with an iron lever.

The interior of the pumphouse, however, was immaculate. Its polished wood, painted iron, whitewashed brick, and shining brass bore witness to the civil engineers who, long after the steam engines were retired by electric ones next door, maintained the old pumphouse and its machinery as a sacred trust. Dallas told us that it had been built not only as a functioning waterworks, but also as a temple to industry. I remember leaving it with the same feelings you might have leaving a church — a church whose god had been austere, severe, beautiful, and Victorian.

Anyway, that fall I went off to study down south and left the steam museum far behind me. When Dad and I returned to it this summer, my work-abroad plans had long since come crashing down around my ears. I was stuck in Canada, the land where nothing happens. Now, Dad's a CPR man, and he and I had actually gone to see working model stream trains that race like greyhounds around an elevated track in the museum grounds. But that day, as I stood in the shadow of the pumphouse, the very fidelity of those pet-sized trains to their panting originals merely underlined the fact that the big steam engines were gone. The grown men who tended to them reminded me only of my own diminished hopes.

So, Dad and I turned to go, when I saw, through the arched windows of the old pumphouse, one of the great flywheels turning. The spokes of the wheel ticked over slowly, as if the building were a titanic watch. Turning from the miniature trains to see that wheel, through arches which echo those of Roman aqueducts, was like turning from nostalgia to resurrection. Still, we got in the car and it wasn't until we were rolling past the pumphouse that Dad stopped, backed up, and in we went. I smiled to see Dallas still there, a stationary curator in the spirit of McFarlane. He quickly joined us up with a tour in progress.

On my first visit, the pumphouse interior had seemed like a church whose god had gone — an ancient god, because the iron pillars supporting the entablature on which the twenty-five-ton rocking beams balance are cast as fluted Doric columns. And fluted, too, is the pump rod — the one the beams moved up and down to draw and push the water, like a great heart, from the bay and halfway up the mountain, to wash down into Hamiltonian homes. This time the guide flicked a switch and, with a hum, one of the beams began to move. It leaned out of the ceiling, the forearm of Apollo, elbowing down from the solid cloud of the whitewashed roof. In the same motion, the trussed rod connecting the beam to the flywheel began revolving those twenty-two tons of arc'd iron. All that was missing was the steam itself to make the pumphouse a living temple.

Chief engineer James McFarlane's desk is still there between the columns, opposite the original entrance, like a pulpit in reverse. Through the wall on the other side of his desk, an organ — the pipes of which were four boilers, each thirty feet long and six feet wide — supplied the steam that drove the engines. Those boilers are gone now, but they, like the walking beams, the flywheels, and all the castings and forgings, were made — not in England, nor even the United States — but in nearby Dundas, by John Gartshore. McFarlane came to work for him at the same time Gartshore landed the contract for the beam engines. McFarlane supervised their construction and then ran them for half a century, living and raising two families on site, a curate engineer.

I went to visit the waterworks a third time, so that I could write this story. Arriving on site alone, I was able to appreciate the pumphouse's classical lines and sober, soaring stone against the sky. Also its 150-foot chimney, which looks like a bell tower, once used by mariners on Lake Ontario to steer their vessels by as they approached Burlington Bay. When Dallas came out of the site office to greet me that morning, he was preceded by a cat. I asked its name.

"Keefer," Dallas replied, after Thomas Keefer, the master engineer whose brainchild the waterworks were. The steam engines are *house built*, meaning they're inseparable from the building that houses them. In keeping with that, the story Dallas told me then, of McFarlane's son, Blair, who rode the walking beams when his father was not around and whose initials are scratched into the wall by his father's desk, humanized the machinery, made it to scale with the people who ran it.

And I thought about my first visit to the steam museum, when real work was done elsewhere. I thought about my father, who'd made his living among steam locomotives. And I thought about what Dallas said the engines would have sounded like, powered by those gone Gartshore boilers: a regular sigh — not loud. Quietly, then, the pumphouse seemed to say, "Your work is here; your labour, here. The materials you need, and the skills to fashion them, are at hand."

At the end of our tour, Dallas took me up to the beam deck, just beneath the roof, and set one of the engines in motion. The walking beam bowed and rose, bowed and rose both, at the same time.

Beggar Waltz

The *Fresh Air* skating party, held before Christmas, just about finished me off. I went to the open-air rink at Nathan Phillips Square to wait for Barb, Adrian, and Jeff to show up after work. I'm not a good skater and it was very cold. So when Jeff clapped an arm on my shoulder and shouted "Your prayers have been answered! Barb and Adrian are sick and the party's cancelled," I was hugely relieved. Jeff and I then moved the skating party to the nearby Rex Tavern, where we inhaled a pack of cigarettes between us, with beer chasers, and shared stories. It turned out to be a great night — with an even better walk home, alone beneath a full moon, through pockets of city parkland that funnel up the night sky. By the next morning, however, all of that huffing and puffing left me gasping for a workout.

So, that evening, I hauled myself toward the downtown Toronto YMCA. Up ahead on Yonge Street, a man was dancing for change on the sidewalk. Every time a person passed close to him, he began singing something I couldn't catch and then, without lifting his feet, went into this little bounce while sticking out his change cup. The sight of him disgusted me. You know how you hate the people you can't help? Well, I really hated this guy. I stalked past him and arrived at the Young Men's Christian Association, where I baptized myself in the pool, solidified myself in the weight room, and did a slow dance of tai chi in an empty squash court. I left feeling like a new man.

At this point, it was so cold out I took the streetcar over to Queen Video to rent some movies. Imagine the consternation of this new man I was when I saw the dancing beggar again. He must have moved across town in the time I'd been exercising. He now stood at Queen and Spadina, doing his shifty bounce, mumble-jumbling, and sticking out his cup. I zombied past him like before. Hadn't the *Globe and Mail* just published a series of articles on homelessness, stating that this streetside hoofer might be making hundreds of dollars a day? Then I rented two films — an old musical called *Follow the Fleet* and the futuristic *Fifth Element* — to make me feel good in my cozy apartment. Cocooned on my couch, I stuck the first movie in my VCR, closed my heart, and opened my eyes.

Follow the Fleet stars Ginger Rogers and Fred Astaire. Virtually all of the Astaire-Rogers films came out of the Depression and this one, especially so. It finishes with a staged vignette Fred and Ginger put on to raise money for a friend, in which Fred plays a gambler who loses all his cash at the tables. Dejected, he goes to the terrace of the casino and approaches the high-society types who, until he was broke, draped his shoulders and egged him on. Now they sashay past him as if his white tie were a black hole. Left alone, Fred raises a gun to his head and is about to pull the trigger when Ginger shows up.

We never know what her trouble is, but as she's about to jump from the deco rooftop in her shimmering metallic gown Fred whips over to her, tails flying, and pulls her from the ledge.

Rescued by his need to rescue her, Fred laughingly shows her his gun. She reaches for it, so he throws it away. Fred then shows her his empty wallet, shrugs, and throws that away too. Then he sings the hopeful dirge "Let's Face the Music, and Dance." Ginger remains frozen with grief. Masked by her porcelain face, she is the doll of the Depression: her eyes full of sorrow, her features empty of expression. Only when Fred begins to cast his dancing spell, reaching to the air on either side of her, does she move.

The next morning, I got moving myself and walked east along Adelaide, my favourite street. After the Astaire-Rogers film, I had watched *The Fifth Element*, so it was hard not to notice the poster of Milla Jovovich's face stretched across a building wall on Adelaide West. In the movie, Milla plays Leeloo, an orange-haired warrior — a valiant, vulnerable vortex of martial dexterity — sent to protect life on earth against a great gob of evil from outer space.

The poster is an ad for L'Oréal. Milla's image gives the oncoming traffic the same killer look Leeloo gave the taunting general in *The Fifth Element* just before she punches through protective glass, grabs him by the tie, and slams his head against the shattered shield. She then busts out, into multi-layered Manhattan, with its streams of airmobiles and vertical commuter trains. The poster makes Milla a more conventional brunette; in the midst of that hair a message reads "Because I'm worth it."

I wonder what messages like that mean to the homeless as they shamble by? The poster is pseudo-signed "Milla Jovovich," but do the folks at L'Oréal expect us to believe she reached up there and personally endorsed this propertied picture? Still, I wanted to believe that, or something like it, for there are no reachings like winter reachings — the poor, the desperate, the dancing for very cold, reach out. They are made desperate in the same way advertisements seek to make us desperate for what they pretend to offer. I wanted to believe Milla's ad mask reached back, that it had some affinity with fiery-haired Leeloo; that it would shatter the unbreakable glass between the lucky and the left-out, and tell them they were worth it too, before busting into a vast metropolis, layered with true charity.

Musing on Milla, and Fred and Ginger, I made my way to the Second Cup on Adelaide at University, had a latté in the warmth, and went up to the Y again — heck, I was on holidays now, why not? Afterwards, as I walked back down Spadina in the sun to return the videos, there was the dancing man. Only, he wasn't bouncing or singing now; the sidewalk was bare as a branch in December, and he hugged a building wall while making his way uptown. I made a bee-line for him. Dipping into my store of hackneyed phrases at the same time as my pocket, I said "Hey, can you use a buck?" He extended his hand and accepted my offering, this hardworking vaudevillian, which was more than I deserved.

You don't get third chances very often in this life. And I know I didn't do anything for that guy by scraping out my change. He rescued me. In winter, the streetside poor become our collective Ginger, with their frozen faces and pealing eyes. It may help to remember, at those cold moments when we stalk past the needy, that even Fred was bypassed. We pass him every day. Hard up on his luck, with his buried dexterity, he waits to cast his spell, to help us face the music of this world, and dance. He does it because ... because we're worth it.

Sky Train

Three years ago, on Easter Saturday, I rode my bicycle from Toronto to my parents' home in Burlington. On the last leg of the journey, I raced a locomotive across a field south of Highway 5 and then flew down Guelph Line, the wind behind me. I arrived, panting and sweaty, at the apartment door. Dad went to tell Mom I was there and then, with a slow creaking, she came down the hall using her walker. She was wearing the Tigger t-shirt I had given her, and when she came up to me, she punched the air in triumph and went "P-kshh!"

That was Mom, in her final season fighting the cancer which had hung on to her for almost a decade. It had not kept her down. For years, she volunteered at the cancer clinic at Joseph Brant Hospital, where she herself had been operated on. She always went to church, remaining a pillar of strength to many throughout her illness, but this Easter, I could see that attending the service was not going to be easy.

I myself did not want to go. As the three of us sat watching the old Easter standby, *Ben-Hur*, I asked Dad if he would drive me back to Toronto with my bike in the trunk of his car. Mom wanted me to stay overnight, and go to church in the morning, but I was hell-bent on getting out of there. Although I didn't say so, the thought of my mother creaking up the aisle of St. Stephen United in her walker was more than I could bear. Dad agreed to take me back and off we went.

Mom and I had watched *Ben-Hur* together when I was a kid. She loved the sea fight and the chariot race, but the scene that always struck me the most was when Ben-Hur's mother and sister are healed of leprosy. After the crucifixion, the wrath of God rips open the sky; lightning topples trees and rain washes Christ's blood all the way to the cave where the two women are sheltering from the storm. They cry out at every stroke, while, with each flash, their disheveled faces appear, clearer and clearer of the disfiguring disease. When I first saw this, I didn't understand why they were weeping and asked Mom what was going on. "It's a miracle," she said.

Mom wasn't expecting a miracle as she sat alone watching *Ben-Hur* after Dad and I left, but as we neared the on ramp of the QEW, I asked him to turn the car around. Something told me I wasn't going to get this chance again. When we both returned about ten minutes later, Mom smiled. The three of us went to church the next morning. As I sat beside Mom during communion, she pressed the hand of another woman who, although very ill, had still been able to go up to the front, as Mom herself could not. As it turned out, that Easter was the last time she was able to get out of the house.

It was also the first of several instances, as Mom entered the last stretch of her life, where it was given me to know when to take the green GO Train, bound for Burlington, to be with her: the last time she walked, the last time she tried to get out of bed, the last moments when she was with us. She had wanted to die at home and, along with help from the Victorian Order of Nurses, Dad tended to her constantly.

My own activities were far less taxing. Mom didn't want to be read to much or even spoken with very often. She wanted, in her own words, to think, something which has made more and more sense to me as time goes on. So I played solitaire on the bed beside her hospital bed, which the Red Cross had loaned us, got her coffee and stroked her forehead, which was, at this point, the only part of her that didn't hurt when touched. "I love it when you do that," she said.

On the morning we knew she was bed-rid, I got into Dad's car and sped off to buy a poster for the wall she was facing. I found something vivid and Mediterranean, full of gold ochres, cobalt, and viridian, called *Sun & Sea*. She loved that, too. It didn't take much to please my mother, as she lay there in her bedroom, preparing for a journey far beyond the water.

I have seen her several times since she left us, always at night, of course, and always in dreams. Most recently, we were on a train bound for Toronto. It was a streamlined train from the final time of steam, when locomotives became more like little skyscrapers laid on their sides than iron-age work horses; when they were for the first time aerodynamic, and for the last time the cutting edge of transportation and progress.

My mother and I were inside one of a line of emerald passenger cars that arc'd away from the marble-clad engine. And I knew, in the way you know things in dreams, that these trains traversed southern Ontario from end to end and, what was even more astounding, they ran on elevated tracks that twisted and turned like rain-wet roads in rural France. On these uplifted rail paths, the massive green steam trains glanced past each other with terrific velocity.

But the main amazement was, each time the engine blew off steam, it clouded from a circular vent that compassed the boiler at the front. With a long, drawn-out "P-kshh," the entire train became enveloped in hot mist. This sheathing of steam was so colossal — the engine was working so hard — that the water of it congealed in the air, making a momentary, humming tunnel through which Mom and I, as awestruck passengers, ran.

I wondered, on waking, why my father had not been with us in the rail car. Then I realized, he was the engine, who had picked me up at the station every time I took the GO Train in, and who picked up my mother so often he ended up getting a hernia. He had carried us both through that cloudy passage, that weeping tunnel, and still carries me, every time I see him, clear out the other side. I have often felt bitter that Mom was denied the cinematic miracle of *Ben-Hur*, that the rage at her dying was not enough to cleanse her of cancer. But surely the miracle remains in how she and Dad tiger'd out the worst. When I think of heaven now, I imagine a network of elevated, emerald trains, in which we are all passing.

NOTES

Engine

Wade in the Water

Broadcast 28 October 2000. The best account of William Ward is in Sally Gibson's *More Than an Island: A History of the Toronto Island*. Bill Freeman has himself written a briefer account in *A Magical Place: Toronto Island and its People*. Sadly, there is as yet no monument to Ward in the city, while the statue of his great contemporary, Ned Hanlan, is now somewhat lost in front of the former Marine Museum in the CNE grounds.

Bathurst Street Bridge

This was my first piece for *Fresh Air*. It was read by Tom Allen at ten to seven one November morning in 1996. Tom prefaced the story by saying "Ward wrote this letter on a bridge which I have taken for granted certainly not less than a thousand times." It was written in the spirit of the prose poems Tom used to conjure up out of thin air at six in the morning.

Summer Stars

Broadcast 23 September 2000. Smit is an archaic, but acceptable, past tense of smite.

Mercer Union

Broadcast May 1997. Mercer Union has moved to 37 Lisgar Street. "The Samuel Building" can still be made out as of this writing, and the carpet is gone!

Rock of Ages

Broadcast 21 April 2001. Margaret Burgess was Frye's co-lecturer and TA when I took the latter's course in 1989. I have never seen a discreet pairing work better in class. Typology, as a method of reality, informs much of my work.

Firebox

Impurvious

Broadcast January 1997. The first floor of the Blockhouse No. 2 (also called the Centre Blockhouse, and referred to on site as the CB) is now the setting for a fine nineteenth-century artillery display, curated by Carl Benn, whose vision and scholarship informs all aspects of the fort as we currently enjoy it. There is no typo in Impurvious.

Green Tigers

Broadcast 27 July 1998. Fort Bogatron is, in fact, a jewel of an historic site, ably interpreted. Barrie and I hit it on an off day, long ago.

Canadian Corps

Broadcast 11 March 1999. I am indebted to Wayne Reeves' *Regional Heritage Features on the Metropolitan Toronto Waterfront*, a report to the Metropolitan Toronto Planning Department, for this article. Reeves' immensely helpful document may stand for the usefulness and needfulness of Metro before it was destroyed forever by the Ontario government.

Isaac's Ladder

Broadcast 23 October 1999. Both Isaac Brock and Superman came from elsewhere (the Isle of Guernsey and Planet Krypton, respectively), but both are Canadian creations, and both wore a lot of red. Matt Mcdonald is a member of Princess Patricia's Canadian Light Infantry. The war horse is in the Book of Job.

Mike's Drum

Broadcast 19 February 2000. Images from the walking tour, taken by Jim Panou, can be seen on the *Fresh Air* website. See the Introduction for more of this story.

Countryside

Foulard Romance

Broadcast 20 February 1998. I am indebted to Michelle Parise, then the producer of *Fresh Air*, for the kick-start to this story (and many others that followed). Having rejected a piece I submitted about building addresses, she said, "I want more Ward." Thanks, Michelle, for authorizing this author.

The Cows Come Home

This piece, approved for content by my mother, was broadcast on Easter Sunday 1997, the last time she was able to attend church. See "Sky Train" for the rest of that story.

Sweeping Gestures

Broadcast 1 May 1999. The Museum of Human Movement came to me in dreamtime, shortly after I left acting school in New York City. The dance curator reappears in "Gotham Lullaby." Everything on the farm actually happened. After I sent this story to Paul, he sent me a photo of the tree whose branches supported the Rock that Turns.

Arbor Vitae

Broadcast 28 November 1998. Peter Asselstine, a colleague at Copp. Clark, is the one who suggested that the stumbly mouse may have been poisoned before its fall.

Prairie Wind

Broadcast 16 June 2001.

Couplings

Dearest Kid

Broadcast 25 November 2000.

Abandoned Love

Broadcast 17 March 2001. Mike Greenspoon gave this story his approval before broadcasting. The cat hardly noticed the turtle.

Darling Building

Broadcast 25 March 2000. Shelley Wall still has a studio on Spadina, although not in the Darling Building. She is making her real and rare way as a representational painter.

Promised Land

Broadcast 10 February 2001.

Ward Story

Broadcast 27 November 1999. This story has been turned into a superb (and funny) web slide show by Dwight Friesen, a webmaster at the CBC, and can be seen at the *Fresh Air* site. *William James' Toronto Views*, published by Lorimer, is a good introduction to James's work. I owe the housing/herd image to Philip Stern.

Sleepers

Bystanding

Broadcast 8 January 1999.

Concourse Building

Broadcast December 1996. The Concourse Building is to be demolished. Oxford Properties' plans to preserve the façade of the lower stories are an insult to the building's appeal as an integrated skyscraper from portal to cornice. At least we all get another glass box to reflect urban gridlock. Oh boy!

Crossing Over

Broadcast August 1997. With thanks to Michelle Dale, archivist of the former Toronto Harbour Commission. The 509 Streetcar now cuts across the entire intersection, a welcome addition to the ongoing confusion.

YMCA!

Broadcast November 1997. Matthew later gave me his laptop, on which most of these stories were written.

Hauling Up Ryerson

Broadcast 12 June 1999. I am no longer with Lorimer, but the portrait is still there. Also, after hearing this story, the architects of 35 Britain Street ensured that "Egerton Ryerson Memorial Building" headed the new signage at the entrance: a more than civil gesture.

Grand Central Station

Movable Type

Broadcast 19 April 1998. This story was presented at a CBC open house marking Radio One's move to 99.1 FM. Accordingly, the writers of *Fresh Air* were asked to write a story on "moving."

Fightmaster

Broadcast 10 September 1998.

Last Call

Broadcast 24 July1999. Richard Bachmann, dean of Canadian booksellers, also snatched up a copy of Mitchell and was quick to tell me of his importance.

Haida

Broadcast 1 July 2000. There is now a fine, illustrated book on the ship called *HMCS Haida: Battle Ensign Flying*, by Barry Gough. Vice-Admiral Harry DeWolf passed on 19 December 2000, at the age of ninety-seven. The production of *The Caine Mutiny Court Martial* that I saw starred Michael Moriarty as Greenwald, and the superb Philip Bosco as Queeg.

Gotham Lullaby

Broadcast 6 January 2001. Randolyn wrote back to ask, "Was I really that serious?" This story misses her sense of humour, as do I.

Steam

Pistons & Plastrons

Broadcast 31 May 1998.

Bar Hopping

Broadcast 3 October 1998. Both Tim and Mychol have moved on to other things. The final dance in *The Sky's the Limit* had a hard time making it past the war censors of the day. Small wonder.

House of Industry

Broadcast 7 September 1999.

Beggar Waltz

Broadcast 15 January 2000.

Sky Train

Broadcast 13 May 2000. Composed almost entirely to Brian Eno's "Deep Blue Day."

INDEX